Posterity of Seth

Hidden Knowledge Series

From the creation myths of some of the oldest cultures around the world.

Merging Myth with Science.

Posterity of Seth

Jodie K. Scales

Writers Club Press
San Jose New York Lincoln Shanghai

Posterity of Seth

Writers Club Press
an imprint of iUniverse, Inc.

For information address:
iUniverse, Inc.
5220 S. 16th St., Suite 200
Lincoln, NE 68512
www.iuniverse.com

ISBN: 0-595-20585-2

Printed in the United States of America

PROLOGUE

Mankind is at a threshold of spiritual transformation. Can the entrance through the veil separating the worlds and leading to transcendence be found?

Amir stands motionless in the lush green of the near rainforest like surroundings. He cannot help but take a few minutes to ponder the wonder of it all as he watches Adar readying the pillar. They both know that the wonders and mysteries they have placed in the pillar will one day be echoed as a great voice of an ancient conscience. They only hope in silence that they have infused the contents with the correct amount of wisdom, power and truth to be understood within the hidden depths of the soul, and used appropriately by those who uncover it in the ages to come.

Three clay tablets, all needed to understand the significance and magnitude of their revelations, six maps of the surveys of the material world's changing crust displacement and their book of creation have all been wrapped separately and secured inside the elaborately decorative four-foot pillar. Amir had carved the four floral swaths that spiraled down and around the fluted center himself. The craftsmanship was exemplary, just as Adar instructed him it should be.

Adar is sure that they are doing the right thing. She has told Amir over and over again that no matter how long the span of mankind lasts, there will always be a light of love lying dormant in their souls. It will be that light that leads the right person to finding the pillar of knowledge they are about to hide within the layers of the earth beneath the lush green forest.

Amir again felt the full weight of the burden of the knowledge he has and the hellish torment that might befall mankind if the pillar is found by the wrong souls. The wretchedness and torment of a destructive power uncovering all that they have encased in the pillar had been haunting him for days and even Adar's reassurances now could not put them to rest. It seemed that a surge of gripping fear began anew to ripple through his body and soul, paralyzing him where he stood. His breath was sucked powerfully from his lungs as a morbid vision immediately overtook him.

The lush green life of the forest around him was transformed to a lifeless, hot, dry desert of sand. Heat rose in an ominous transparent manner causing Amir to squint to maintain his vision. All life was gone and had been for a very long time. Under his feet, where thick green grass had grown was now only hot gritty grains of sand. There was nothing for miles but more of the same lifeless dry desolation.

Suddenly a thunderous voice became a part of the surreal experience confronting Amir. It was a scolding devilish voice that Amir immediately knew to be the voice of Ialdabaoth. Amir was again paralyzed by the whirlwind of Ialdabaoth's scolding declarations. Even when the ground Amir stood on seemed to be opening up into a cavernous abyss he could not move. The horrific vision was accompanied by an acrid, nausea-inducing stench penetrating the still air around Amir. The foul-smelling pit that lay open beneath his feet was alive with hideously grotesque images wallowing in their own wretchedness.

Amir had turned an ashy white and was covered with sweat when Adar had finished readying the pillar and looked up toward him. She knew immediately that he must be in the grip of Ialdabaoth and that she would have to act quickly. She ran across the lush green padding of the forest floor, each step bringing her closer to the danger that had engulfed Amir. Without thinking Adar jumped powerfully with her arms stretched out before her. The power of her forward motion caused the impact to shake her very being. She felt the pain of contact through her shoulders and down into her chest. Still the pain was a small price to pay for forcibly knocking Amir from the vision Ialdabaoth had trapped him in. Amir fell backwards to the green cover of the forest floor. The gripping fear that had paralyzed Amir no longer had a full hold on him, yet he was still physically unsettled and unsure of the wisdom of their plans. Time unknowingly slipped by as Adar reminded Amir of the importance of their task. Before they realized it, the sun was beginning to set and they know they had no choice but to finish what they had come to this very location in the forest to do.

CHAPTER I

The auditorium was full as was accustomed for the first introductory lecture of Dr. Emrys' fall class. It always amazed Cordie that so many students registered for her class and then shied away from the real challenge of her teachings. As she entered from the side door she knew that only a handful of the mass of students would still be with her come the end of the term. It had kind of become a game she and Adam played to see if they could determine which students would last through the first massive round of withdrawals after her initial class introduction. Adam Khalid had been her teaching assistant nearly 6 years ago and was now a young professor assigned to her department at the prestigious Christian Ivy League graduate school in upper New York. Adam was by far the sharpest student and colleague Cordie had ever worked with and they had become great friends as well as professional partners. They dinned together at one of the dozen or so low-key cafes around the campus at least twice a week. Adam was one of the few men that Cordie had ever invited inside her sparkly decorated apartment just a few blocks off campus. For the most part Cordie was a reserved and very private person who seemed to enjoy her solitude.

Dr. Emrys handed a stack of papers to Adam as she walked past on her way up the three narrow stairs to the main stage floor of the huge auditorium. On the top of the stack was a hand written note that simply read "No more than 2/3rds". Adam smiled as he read it and added his own prediction immediately below it.

The low heals of her conservative black pumps made an echoing sound as they hit the bare wood of the stage floor. Either the sound of her approaching the microphone, or simply her presents on the stage, served to quiet the restless students and draw their attention to her small frame, alone amidst the emptiness of the large stage. Adam watched with a slight smile of satisfaction, as the entire auditorium quieted and everyone gave their attention to Dr. Cordelia Emrys.

Adam hit the light control panel and darkened the room, leaving only a soft ray of light cascading directly down on Dr. Emrys and the single microphone positioned in the center of the stage. Even more of a hushed attention fell over the entire auditorium as all attention was now completely focused on the poised and well-prepared Dr Emrys as she began to speak.

"A place to begin, as with all things the real origin of any beginning must be with God. God the Creator, God the Alpha and Omega, GOD." Dr. Emrys paused for affect then in the same confident and commanding manner went on. "So from what perspective shall we look to God for our beginning? For the purposes of this class, I am going to narrow the choices in which you may answer that very important question down to only two possibilities; a *religious* perspective or a *scientific* perspective."

Adam had heard her introduction more than a dozen times yet he never tired of hearing it again. He was just as intrigued by her soft demur presents and the delivery of her class introduction and ideas as he was the first time he had heard her. He had never known anyone else who could bring a disappearing world to vibrant life the way Cordie seemed to do. He remembered how her words had set his mind racing trying to catch all of the implications of what she was saying when he had been a student setting in the same auditorium. She had set his mind free from conventional belief and allowed him to embrace the previously inconceivable. Having been raised in a conservative Christian family in the

Midwest, Adam had never questioned creation. It wasn't that he completely disregarded evolution but he simply knew that God had created everything and therefore Adam had never asked himself the tuff questions that Dr. Emrys demanded be asked of each of her students.

"Having drawn much of my information for this class and thesis of study from many disciplines of science, Astronomy, Astrology, Anthropology, Archeology, Paleontology and Geology just to mention a few, I would have a very difficult time leaving out any perspective that did not include one of a scientific nature." Dr. Emrys continued. "However, just as the many different disciplines of science overlap and many times take the same subject matter and look at it from differing angles, any look at God must naturally include the religious perspective. Therefore we will endeavor to look at God and our beginning from both a scientific and a religious perspective. I must also tell you at this point that the religious perspective will cover both religion and what many may deem even more significant, spirituality. As you will see, religion is a group belief set down in specific guidelines where as spirituality is a personal issue of the soul."

Dr. Emrys moved slightly to one side and the light followed her. She effortlessly continued, "Science seeks to answer the technicalities of *how* something operates or works in a mechanistic fashion. Whereas religion seeks to answer the human concerns of a relationship with God and seeks to answer theologically *why* were our world and we created. Using a Christian basis to further explain this point, the Bible is not intended as a scientific, how God created the universe out of nothingness, but rather a lesson about people's relationship with God from the time that he created the universe out of nothingness. I believe it is very possible to have a truly Christian, biblically based perspective of our beginnings and creation that stands along side and is a part of a scientific explanation of how. My attempt will be to take you on a journey of exploratory thought and look at our origins, our beginning, by looking at all of the available sources of science and religion while keeping them each in

their intended and correct context. Note here that I have very intention-
ally labeled this class as a journey of "exploratory thought". If any of you
are here because you are expecting an Indiana Jones or Lara Croft,
Tomb Raider type journey, I am afraid you will be very surely disappointed." Dr Emrys raised her arms into the air, took one step to the
side of the microphone and said with a charming smile, "As you can
easily determine, I am not Lara Croft and I can assure you that Dr.
Khalid is no Indiana Jones."

Dr. Emrys waited for the slight laughter of the students to quiet and
then continued. "Just as I have used a number of differing scientific disciplines I have also collected, studied and compared many religions in
addition to Christianity. It is clear to me that just as we can see a more
complete scientific answer to how by using many of the differing scientific disciplines, we can see a more complete answer to why by using the
information found in many religions. That is not to suggest that we are
looking at many Gods." Dr Emrys paused again for effect and then very
powerfully said, "Let me be perfectly clear on that point. It is my belief
that there is only one God, God the creator and that God is supreme
and without equals or competitors. We may look at God as being called
by a variety of names, but there is only one God."

She shifted back just a bit to center her petite frame behind the microphone once again and continued in her soft but strongly competent
voice, "Each religion that we look at will have some significance in our
search for understanding our relationship with God and the similarities
of the varied religions on our understanding of that God. It was this one
God who created everything from nothingness and it is God that we
should trust, worship and serve not the creations of God nor man.

Probably the most debatable aspect of this class is going to be in my
delivery of a theory on the age of man and God's creation of our universe rather than whether I am presenting it from a scientific or religious
perspective. Again, using many scientific areas of study and the creation
myths and believes of many different religious foundations I believe that

I can and have within the framework of this class, shown that we as a people, humanity created in God's own image, was on this earth long long before most people believe. Not only did human existence thrive, but highly developed intelligent civilizations with knowledge that has been lost that may have far excided our present level of understanding existed prior to what we have been taught was the earth's prehistory."

Adam looked around the still darkened auditorium for movement. It had not been unheard of in years past to have at least a few of the students be sufficiently incensed at this point of the introduction to get up and walk out. It had taken young Adam several terms to build up the unaffected confidence in the class material not to be hurt by the rejection of Dr. Emrys theories by so many of the students.

Dr. Emrys continued, "There are far too many examples of unexplained knowledge existing within cultures and during periods of time in which that knowledge was not believed to have existed yet. There are ancient connections linking otherwise unrelated civilizations that have never been successfully explained. Similarities in the founding principals of religions among people who had supposedly never had contact with each other and the common elements in the creation myths of similarly isolated cultures will begin to give you cause for reexamining your believes. How else can the striking similarities of legendary civilizations spoken of in nearly all of the mythologies of the world be explained?

Then examples of detailed maps of parts of the earth not even discovered at the time of the maps, or construction that has been based on complex understandings of the size of the earth and it's relationship to the stars will, I believe, help you come to terms with the concept of a much more distant beginning than you may have ever imagined. These examples could easily be evidence of the ancient secrets surrounding us that are now demanding to be told. Along with that concept you may also begin to realize that it is quite possible and even probable that human knowledge and civilization has not developed in a linear fashion as previously believed.

Civilization has not developed from a primitive chaos to our current state of order and knowledge in one progressive path.

Instead, knowledge and civilization may very well have cycled through entire epochs since the creation of the human race. The ancient Aztecs believed that the universe had cycled through four previous stages or suns, placing them as well as our current population in the Fifth Sun. Each previous Sun had reached a varied level of advancement and then was totally or nearly totally wiped out by some form of catastrophe. Each new Sun began with none or only a portion of the knowledge achieved by the previous, completely disproving the concept of a steady linear path of knowledge and development."

Adam hit the appropriate switch on the control panel and the lights gradually came back up. He could see both the look of intrigue and the look of complete dissatisfaction on the faces of the still quiet student audience. Dr. Emrys smiled and looked up from her notes as she took the microphone from its stand and moved closer to the front of the stage. She spoke into the hand held microphone, "Don't let me stop with merely setting the seed of disbelieve in your minds. For those of you willing to seriously study and put to challenge the current believes that you have in relationship to creation, evolution, and the history of our existence as human beings, I put forth yet another area of thought that we will explore in this class, How much 'time' was taken for creation? What is time? Did God create *slowly* or did He create everything in a moment of time? Would He have created our environment and given it an appearance of age it didn't have?

In this class you will learn just how significantly the Theory of Relativity has forever changed our concept of Time. You will be challenged and made aware of the passage of time that connects us even as it separates us." Dr. Emrys concluded and without any further delay returned the hand held microphone to its stand, turned and walked slowly toward the exit.

Adam left his position behind the light control panel and stood squarely at the front corner of the auditorium. "Dr. Emrys will be available for individual questions or comments in her office each week according to the schedule you have each received. Our first class will meet tomorrow beginning with a presentation of the theory of The Fifth Sun as presented in the Vaticano-Latin Codex. Please have read the material and be prepared to participate in Dr. Emrys' discussion of the topic." He concluded as Cordie continued walking off the stage and out again through the side door.

CHAPTER 2

"Dr. Emrys, Dr. Cordielia Emrys?" a somewhat hurried voice called out after Cordie. "Please, Dr Emrys if I could have but just a moment of your time."

Cordie turned around to look over her shoulder, in the almost disserted hall, expecting to see one of the students from her lecture who just couldn't wait to tell her either how completely ludicrous her class must be, or how wonderful they thought her ideas were. It was always one or the other, one extreme to the other, never just a simple educational curiosity that one might have for, oh say a traditional history or literature class. She had reluctantly slowed and turned to see instead a small frail looking man of nearly 80 or so running after her. He was wearing a fine impeccably tailored three-piece suite, even more conservative than her own attire and it was apparent that he was not from the school, let alone her class.

"Dr. Emrys, oh thank you, thank you for stopping, I was afraid I was going to miss you and we have such little time my dear!" the old man continued rambling on as he took Cordie's arm and began walking with her back toward her office.

"Excuse me sir, I don't believe we have been introduced and what do you mean that we have such little time?" Cordie replied politely but with question in her tone. She felt as if she had somehow stumbled into a strange version of *Alice in Wonderland* and had just encountered the mad hatter or rabbit spouting off about being late for a very important date.

"Oh my, oh my I have begun all wrong, I am afraid. You would think that at my age I would be better at presenting myself. Please excuse my hast my dear, I am Felix Smith and it is so very important that we talk privately. I am sure that you will find what I have to tell you of great interest and unfortunately I must insist that it be right now. I'll explain it all, just as soon as we are alone in your office." the old man spoke in such a quick and hushed voice that Cordie was beginning to be drawn in by the intrigue his presents suggested.

"Very well Mr. Smith, here we are." Professor Emrys said as she turned the key in her office door. Pushing open the heavy wooden door Cordie slid one arm inside and turned on the light switch. "Please, come in and tell me what has you in such a state."

As she moved behind her large wooden desk as she always did upon entering her small unimpressive office, Cordie watched the old man look curiously around the room. His eyes darted around the room as if he was looking for someone or something specific. His frail looking arm reached back behind himself and pushed the door closed. Cordie thought he was acting very strangely, but she didn't think at his age he was of any danger to her. She made herself comfortable in the large desk chair and waited for Mr. Smith to turn his attention back to her.

As had been expected, Adam heard several students already discussing their plans to drop this ridiculous class as they left the auditorium. It always amazed him how close minded people could be, especially about things that might threaten their believe systems. It angered him enough when he heard one athletic looking young man comment on his way past the front table, "Next she'll be trying to convince us that we all come from little green space men" that Adam was about to open his mouth in defense of Professor Emrys when something else attracted his attention.

"Excuse me, Professor Khalid" a soft yet confident voice broke into his thoughts. "I am sorry to bother you with this right away, however, it is quite important to me. Does Dr. Emrys have any flexibility concerning the class schedule?"

The enchanting sound of the voice was so tantalizing and somehow familiar but Adam could not place it. He looked up to see the most attractive young woman he believed he had ever laid eyes on. She was tall and slender with long dark hair and almost black eyes that seemed to pierce through him. He must have been staring because she tilted her head sideways and gave him a very peculiar smile.

"I don't mean to sound difficult from the very beginning, but I may have somewhat of a conflict with a small portion of the class schedule and I am wondering if Dr. Emrys is the type that might allow me to work it out so that I may take the class." the young woman went on to explain.

"Oh, and you are?" Adam asked trying to recover from his boyish stupidity. He couldn't understand the immediate attraction he felt for this young student. It wasn't like him at all to be taken so by a student, no matter how attractive she might be.

"Forgive me, I am Gabriella and I would really hate to have to withdraw from this class. I have read everything that Dr. Emrys has published, not that she has published nearly as much she should have. I am very interested in her research. Taking this class seemed like the best way to get a stronger understanding of her theories."

"Then you are not a regular student her at the University?" Adam inquired.

"No Dr. Khalid, I already have my graduate degree. I am here at the University only for this class."

"Well, Gabriella, what kind of flexibility do you think you would need?" Adam asked in an effort to sound professional and competent.

Gabriella wasn't exactly sure just how much she wanted to reveal to Professor Khalid right away, but he did seem to be a reasonable young man who despite Dr. Emrys' somewhat comical reference to him not being any Indiana Jones, she thought might be interested in her situation. It was just that her grandfather had told her that she must absolutely not tell anyone about their plans ahead of time. "Well," she finally replied with a less than confident tone of voice, "I have a family obligation that will take me out of the country for about two weeks right in the middle of the term."

"Oh, I see how that would be of a concern to you. It is highly irregular to expect to miss a full two weeks of class and still be able to meet all the requirements of the class at this level of study. Is the obligation not something that can be rearranged?" Adam said as he continued to look at the timeless beauty of the young woman standing so near that he could smell the freshness of her perfume and realizing that if he forced her to drop the class he might never have the opportunity to smell anything so enticing again. He didn't know why, but this very moment in time seemed like a defining moment of greatest significance to Adam.

"No, I am afraid that there is no flexibility on the time needed for this particular family obligation." Gabriella's disappointed voice interrupted Adam's thought. "Do you believe that Dr. Emrys will allow me to continue in the class?"

Adam tried desperately not to be too obvious about his instant attraction to Gabriella by hesitating and not being too awfully quick to reassure her that he thought he could intercede on her behalf and convince Dr. Emrys to make an allowance for her. There wasn't a chance that Adam was going to go through the whole term kicking himself for letting Gabriella slip out of his life before he even had a chance to get to know her.

Mr. Smith had finally stopped pacing around Dr. Emrys' office as if he was in search of some hidden danger. He now stood looking out the small window at Dr. Emrys' somewhat pathetic view. She was the only senior faculty member not to have an office overlooking either the small campus lake or the wooded expanse beyond the gardens. Dr.

Cordielia Emrys had only a view of a small cherry tree struggling for attention among the larger oaks leading to the south parking lot of the Milroy building. It was only at times like this, when someone new took the time to stare out her office window that it bothered her anymore. After all, there were some advantages to having an out of the way office. She was rarely interrupted by the goings on of her fellow faculty members and had plenty of privacy. And after all, she was lucky to have found any credible school that would take her on after all of the controversy of her past life.

"Mr Smith," Cordie began in an attempt to draw the strange old man's attention from the window. "You said something about not having a lot of time."

"You are so correct my dear. Let me get on with it and tell you what I have come to talk with you about. I just know that this is going to be more exciting to you than almost anyone else on this earth." Mr Smith's enthusiasm seemed to bring some kind of youthful energy to the old man's face as he moved over to stand in front of Cordie's cluttered desk. He planted both of his aged and bony hands firmly in the center of an uneven stack of papers on her desk and leaned as far across towards her as his small body would allow.

"We have found the original maps." Felix Smith whispered with delight.

Cordie didn't have the slightest idea as to what Mr. Smith was talking about. She shook her head slightly to indicate her confusion and to her surprise the old man broke into laughter.

"The maps my dear. THE maps." He continued through a deliriously joyous laughter, "the original source maps most assuredly those used by Piri Reis, Oronteus Finacus and probably even Mercator and Buache."

Dr. Cordielia Emrys allowed her instinct to take over. She stood quickly making no attempt to stop her desk chair from falling backward against her office wall. It was only the loud bang of the heavy chair hitting the wall that shook Cordie from the state of shock that she had been thrown into.

"I don't know who you are Mr. Smith, or why you have come here today but I assure you."

"I am not an old coot nor crazy here to torment you." Mr. Smith interrupted. "I assure you young lady that I know exactly what I am talking about. I am one of the three people alive that have seen the source maps and we want you to become the fourth. We need your unique perspective to help us unravel the mysterious knowledge that finding these maps seems to have begun bringing to light. Now, are you ready to retrieve your chair and take what I have to say seriously?" The old man now seemed to speak with a new tone of authority.

Before Cordie could respond, Adam pushed open the door with his back and spun around with both hands full of the stacks of papers he had cleaned up from the auditorium. "Oh, pardon me Dr. Emrys, I didn't realize you had a visitor." Adam said slightly embarrassed that he had not knocked before entering her office. He was normally much more polite, but he had not really stopped thinking of how incredibly gorgeous he thought Gabriella was and how much he was looking forward to seeing her face in class each day.

"No, don't be silly." Cordie said, never taking her eyes off the strange old man still leaning across her desk. "Please, Dr. Khalid, come in and just add those to the other stacks here on my desk."

"Ah, Dr. Khalid, allow me to introduce myself young man." Mr. Smith said pleasantly as he straightened up and extended his hand toward Adam.

Adam set the papers among the others on Cordie's desk and reached out to shake the older gentleman's hand.

"I had hoped to meet you on this visit, it is only natural that Dr. Emrys would want to include you in on this project." Felix Smith went on to control the situation with ease. "Could we please close the door young man? This is not the kind of information that we can afford to have become common knowledge, just yet."

Adam was taken back by Mr. Smith and finally noticed the disturbed expression on Cordie's face. Just as Cordie had earlier experienced, Adam began to feel that Mr. Smith was quite an odd character, but didn't seem to fear any danger from him. He did as had been suggested and closed the heavy wooden door.

"Yes Adam, please come in, let's all set down and talk about what Mr. Smith has come to discus with me." Cordie said calmly as she finally did retrieve her chair and allow herself to fall back into it. "You are going to be very interested in his claims."

Adam took a small folding chair from the corner of the office and positioned himself at the end of Cordie's desk, between her and Mr. Smith. It took a few more moments for Mr. Smith to take his seat, but he eventually did. Adam looked questioningly at Cordie then back again at the finely dressed old man.

"Very well, let me begin by providing some background on my credentials so as to give some credibility to my repeated claim to have found the source maps most likely used by Piri Reis in 1513 and Oronteus Finacus in 1531 when they drew accurate maps of the continent of Antarctica before it had even been discovered, let alone depicting it during two very different periods of time when it was not yet covered with ice." Mr. Smith said condescendingly.

Adam looked toward Cordie as he said as politely as possible, "Mr. Smith, both Dr. Emrys and I are very familiar with both the Piri Reis and Oronteus Finacus maps."

"Please don't interrupt me young man. As I was about to explain, I have been researching background information for some of the most well known archeologists and scientific minds of our age for more than 60 years. There probably isn't anyone more comfortable in the Vatican archives or the forgotten reassesses of the Imperial Library of Constantinople in Istanbul than myself. My grandfather and his grandfather before him have all continued our family quest for knowledge through the efforts of our foundation, The Legacy Houses."

Both Dr Emrys and Dr. Khalid turned to stare at each other in amazement. There wasn't anyone in the scientific community that didn't know of The Legacy House foundation. It was as solid and respectable as they come and Adam even began to recall that the original name of the founding family of The Legacy House was Smith.

"Unfortunately, it was Dr. Heath Conrad who originated the find that led us to the source map information, so he is one of the other two I earlier mentioned." Felix went on.

Both Adam and Cordie knew all too well why any involvement on the behalf of the infamous Heath Conrad would be preceded by any reputable scientist with the word unfortunately. At age 44 Heath Conrad had made more enemies within the scientific community than most people could in a full lifetime. He was a talented archeologist and well respected authority on megalithic architecture until the controversy began with his raids on several significant South American sites. Cordie had first met Dr. Conrad during her past life among the ruins of Labaantum, in Belize in Central America. Cordie could not help but wonder just how much of her past this strange Mr. Smith was aware of. Did he know of her involvement with Dr. Heath Conrad all those years ago?

Although Adam had never actually met Dr. Conrad, he trusted what he had read and what little Cordie had told him about the recklessness of the man. He had only heard Cordie speak ill of a handful of people and it was always in a professional manner. He recalled the few times that Dr. Conrad had appeared in the news since he had been working with Cordie and her refusal to discus him. All she would ever say was that some people are best kept at a distance.

"I have come to New York specifically to ask you Dr. Emrys to join our very small team in deciphering the source maps and the multiple implications of the lost knowledge they represent. Again, unfortunately there seems to be a time crunch. I can't go into all of the details at this moment, however, because of the precise alignment of certain sites with the differing planet positions and the delicate nature of these finds, we must have the information deciphered as completely and as quickly as possible. Your expertise could be invaluable to our efforts Dr. Emrys." Felix felt a bit of concern over not having been completely honest about the need for urgency. He preferred to be honest but there really wasn't any good way to explain at this point that the maps were dissolving at an alarming rate.

Cordie and Adam set in amazement looking at each other in what could very easily have been considered a state of shock. Felix wasn't even sure that they realized he had stopped speaking. The late afternoon sun was beginning to hide behind the tree coverage outside Cordie's small window and the office light was fading.

After a few moments of silence it was Adam who next spoke. "You mentioned three, who besides yourself and Dr. Conrad would be included in this small team of yours?"

Cordie couldn't believe her ears. After being told that information truly existed that might prove all of the theories of her scoffed at class and completely rewrite history as it has been known, all Adam could ask was who the third scientist was. She was about to speak when Felix Smith's voice sounded out enthusiastically again.

"Well, that young man is something of a personal secret and not of real relevance to the issues at hand. Let me just tell you at this point that the third member is not of renown scientific recognition and is more a representative of The Legacy House than that of a scientific area of specialty. What should be of importance to both of you at the moment is whether I have enough evidence to support my claims and convince you to quite literally drop off the face of the earth, or at lease disappear from your lives as you know them and go into isolation to solve these mysteries."

"Us," Adam said cautiously, "I don't want to sound ungrateful, but I can of course understand why you would be interested in having Dr. Emrys on your team…I am just wondering what it is that you think I could add?"

"Modesty isn't something you find much of in our circles Dr. Khalid. It is somewhat refreshing but completely unnecessary. Your early work on ancient languages and support of the ideas put forth by Dr. Emrys makes you of quite significant value to our efforts. It is my hope that you will both be on my plane with me this evening."

"This evening!" Cordie finally spoke, "You can not possible expect that we could just leave with you this evening. We have just begun a new term and there isn't anyone on staff that could take over our class." Adam had never heard quite that very mixture of fascination and fear in Cordie's voice.

Mr. Felix Smith stood and no longer looked frail to either Cordie or Adam as he very powerfully insisted, "Yes, in less than five hours to be precise. This is the chance of a lifetime, no, even more than that. This is an opportunity to embark on the adventure of many lifetimes but it must happen tonight. Now are you with us, or not?"

It was not really a question; Mr. Felix Smith knew the frenzy of the scientific mind far too well to have any doubts about either of them taking him up on his offer. Both Dr. Cordielia Emrys and young Dr. Adam Khalid's lives had just changed dramatically.

CHAPTER 3

Adam was still in somewhat of a state of shock as he entered the main conference room of the private jet Felix had instructed both he and Cordie to report to. He had offered to pick Cordie up on his way to the airport, but with such little time she had suggested that they each make whatever final details possible and just meet up at the airport. He was relieved to see that she was already on board when he arrived.

Cordie was setting comfortably behind a lap top computer already entering data into a program that Felix had set up for her. Adam had never seen her look so youthful and totally involved in what she was doing. She had replaced her dark conservative suit and low healed black pumps with comfortable docker pants, a soft light yellow t-shirt and a rather worn pair of very expensive climbing boots. In all of their years together Adam realized that he had never seen Cordie in anything other than her teaching attire. Even on their somewhat regular dinner dates, she had always worn her dark conservative teaching suits. Her long hair was hanging loose around her face and shoulders and he realized that she was not nearly as old as he had previously considered her to be. In fact it flashed through Adam's thought that he really knew very little about his dear friend Cordie, other than what he knew of her from their work in the classroom.

"You must be young Adam," a strong friendly voice sounded from behind. "Come in and let me show you to your quarters before Felix puts you to work as well."

Adam turned to face the warm smile of a tall young man. There was something strangely familiar about his smile and dark eyes, but Adam was sure that he had not met the young man before. He stood a good six inches taller than Adam but looked to be at least a few years younger.

"I am Bruce, Felix is my grandfather and I am kind of the unofficial steward or porter among this scientifically prestigious group. Our flying home doesn't run its self you know." The young man teased as he reached out and took Adam's largest suitcase. "Follow me and I'll show you were to unpack before grandfather realizes you are on board and puts you to work on the language database."

Adam didn't hesitate. There was something about Bruce that he already liked and as eager as he was to begin contributing something to this adventure, it would be nice to see what his quarters were going to look like.

"Now that I have you all together," Felix began as everyone took their designated seats around the large oval conference table in the center of the main cabin of the jet, "let me give you all a short briefing on where we are, and where we are going."

There was no longer any hint of the hurried old man that had initially approached Cordie. Felix Smith was definitely in control and fully aware of the impact of his words and actions. Somehow he seemed wise and trustworthy as he spoke and his way was confidant yet very subtle and unassuming. There was an element of the mysterious to him yet it was so completely masked with his calm, peaceful mannerisms that only someone very observant would even notice it.

There were eight comfortably padded leather seats in all around the impressive oak table. Each had an individual lap top computer positioned directly in front of the person assigned to that seat. Adam had changed into a pair of jeans and t-shirt and was beginning to feel comfortable. He had been assigned the first seat on the left side of the table next to Cordie. The chair to his right set at one of the two ends of the table and was currently not occupied. On the left side of Cordie Bruce was positioned behind his own laptop. Adam still couldn't put his finger on it, but he just felt like he had met Bruce before.

Felix stood behind the chair at the other end of the table as he continued to speak. "We will be taking off shortly and our first destination will be a short stop over in Scotland on our way to Cairo. Although we have a great deal to accomplish before we leave Cairo our entire party will not be able to be assembled until just prior to our departure for South America. We will pick up Dr. Conrad and an assistant he has asked us to include in the group in Scotland. A young man will join us in Cairo who I will introduce you to at that point and of course my other guest will be the last to arrive just prior to our departure."

"It sounds like we are going to be world travelers." Bruce said light heartedly.

"Well now son, that in fact we are. At this point I can simply confirm that we will only be in Scotland long enough to pick up Dr. Conrad and his assistant. Our work really begins when we reach Cairo. Amehd, the young man joining us there is already working on deciphering some of the more difficult elements of the maps we have found and making arrangements to get us access to some of the locations we believe we need to follow up on. We will spend the next several weeks in Egypt and have just enough time to position ourselves in the appropriate locations in South America once our final team member has joined us.

Now each of you will have an area of specialty but I believe that it is extremely important that we interact daily on our progress. This is too important to miss something because we are too narrowly focused."

Felix moved around and took his seat just seconds before the captain's voice announced that they had been cleared for take off. "Buckle up everyone, we should be in the air very shortly"

"Now that that interruption is out of the way," Felix continued, "Adam you will find several of the most sophisticated language programs available on your laptop. You have a direct link into The Legacy House computer banks and we have fed the problem areas of the source maps into your primary drive.

Cordie, you will find equally detailed information on the customs, cultures and mythical databases and resources available through The Legacy House and the Vatican archival libraries. If there is anything else you need, do not hesitate to let me know.

I am sure that you have all met my grandson Bruce by now. I am equally sure that in his modest manner he did not share with you that he is our geological expert. In an effort not to give away more that I should about our adventure at this point, let me just say that the geological knowledge we are going to need on this endeavor is going to be far greater than most would even begin to understand."

"Oh great, grandfather, way to put the pressure on." Bruce jested.

Felix smiled warmly at his grandson and continued on, "Amehd is an astronomical and mathematical expert and I am sure you will all find him a pleasant addition. I don't think I need to say too much about Dr. Conrad and I can't really say much about his assistant as I do not know who he has selected."

Cordie felt her face flush just a bit and hoped that it was only her imagination and that it wasn't apparent to anyone else that she was reacting to the mention of Dr. Conrad. She hadn't thought of him in years and hated the idea of being put in a position where she would actually have to be working with him now. Surely, Felix must have been aware of their past together. Well, it didn't really matter now; she wouldn't have given up the chance to examine original source maps from a prehistory civilization even if it had meant working with the devil himself. And Heath Conrad was in her estimation the closed thing on earth to such a demon.

"I am sorry to interrupt Mr. Smith." The captain's voice sounded again over the cabin intercom system, "we have reached our cruising altitude and it is fine to turn back up the computer equipment as you see fit. We should have a smooth flight of about 9 hours to Glasgow."

"Well, you heard the man, I'll stop talking and each of you can get in at least a few hours of work before turning in." Felix said as he detached his seat belt and stood.

"Wait a minute Mr. Smith!" Cordie sounded nearly speechless with disbelief, "When are we going to see the source maps for ourselves?"

"Good question!" Bruce added with a slight laugh, "I haven't even been privileged enough to see the real things yet."

"Nor will any of you, until we reach Egypt. The portions of the maps that are significant to each of you in your own area of work are loaded into your laptops, but the actual source maps can not be transported and await our arrival in Egypt." Felix said as he turned confidently and left the conference cabin.

After only a few moments of casual conversation all three of the remaining group were drifting into there own state of isolation as they began exploring the information prepared for them on their laptops.

Cordie could hardly contain her amazement, as her computer screen seemed to come alive, tantalizing her every nerve ending as thoughts raced through her mind. She was looking at several views of a very ancient looking clay tablet. It was even older than those she had examined when studying the Samarian legends of Gilgimesh. She recognized the content immediately. There were two parallel straight lines running vertically down the clay tablet. The two lines looked to be approximately seven inches apart with a third line, also etched into the clay tablet vertically and of almost the exact length as the lines on either side, directly down the middle. There was a symbol at the top end of the diagram with another symbol in nearly the same position at the bottom of the diagram. A dot was positioned about an inch to the south of the northern end of the diagram on the center parallel line. Two more lines etched diagonally down from that point reached out to the northern ends of the two outermost parallel lines. The parallel lines were linked directly with slightly lighter etchings of horizontal lines running east to west at the northern and southern ends of the diagram. She knew that she was looking at what was probably the oldest geometrical map of Egypt to ever exist. It had been repeated by numerous generations in an effort to show a simplified geometric concept of the Nile delta with the Great Pyramid resting at the point of the dot, the apex of the Nile delta.

The implications of finding such a clay tablet were very fascinating, but this surely couldn't be the what Felix believed to be the source maps used by ancient generations to map out land masses of the earth not suppose to have been known of during their lifetime. There had to be more that just this. Cordie was just about to open her mouth to ask Adam his opinion when she looked up from her monitor and saw Bruce watching her.

"I am sorry, I don't mean to stare at you Dr. Emrys. It is just that you haven't taken your eyes off that screen for hours. I was wondering if you would even notice if the plane landed." Bruce said softly.

His comments caused Cordie to look around and realize that Adam had already left and she had not even heard him do so. She glanced down at her watch and had to smile back up at Bruce. She has spent nearly four hours studying each view of the clay tablet and the time had passed like no more than a few minutes. Besides, Bruce was such a naturally likable young man that she couldn't not smile back at him.

"Please, as much time as we are going to be spending together, don't you agree we should stay on a first name basis. I am simply Cordie and how long have you been setting there watching me mesmerized over this find?" she said also in a whisper soft voice.

"Only for about the last 45 minutes since Adam finally pulled himself away from his terminal and headed off to bed. He very politely told you good night, but it was apparent that you were in a world of your own.

So have you figured it out yet?" Bruce asked as he handed Cordie a fresh glass of ice water.

"Thank you, and yes it is pretty obvious to me that this tablet represents the Nile valley and delta, but I am sure you and your grandfather already knew that much."

"Yes, your correct but isn't it incredible to find such an accurate representation from such an ancient source. I couldn't help but watch the pleasure on your face as you examined it. After all of these years to finally be on the verge of proving the validity of your life's work must be just incredible. You know, that is what you are about to do. I mean prove everything you have always believed to be true, that human existence goes back hundreds of thousands of years into the past and that great civilizations flourished with knowledge that has been lost to us. Well, at least lost to us until now." Bruce still spoke softly but he simply could not hide his excitement.

It finally began to hit Cordie. She allowed herself to fall limply back into the comfortable leather chair that she had been setting more on the edge of and let out her breath. Could this charming young man be right? Was she about to realize all she had ever dreamed of and if so, what was that going to mean to the world?

CHAPTER 4

Cordie wiped the sleep from her tired eyes and tried her best to look somewhat alert as she set up on her bed. She was still wearing what she had been the evening prior and hadn't even taken the time to turn down the comforter on her bed. She must have fallen asleep as soon as her head had hit the pillow. She remembered thinking that she would just lay down for a few minutes and then change and try to get a bit more research done before they landed in Scotland.

"I hate to wake you, Bruce told me you didn't leave your terminal until only a few hours ago, but I have cleared us through customs and we are nearly ready to head out." Felix said in a nurturing tone from just outside her cabin door.

"Oh, Felix, please come in. I am fully dressed, even if it is in the same cloths I wore last evening." Cordie mumbled almost to her self as she tried to more fully wake herself.

Felix opened her cabin door and stepped just inside. For just a moment or two Cordie felt a bit disorientated. Then she realized that she had nearly forgotten just how elderly Felix was. In the bright light of the morning sun shining in the plane windows Cordie remembered her first impressions of Felix when he had approached her in the university corridor only yesterday. This morning he seemed even older. She couldn't help but noticed his aged and wrinkled skin hanging loosely on the bones of his fingers as he raised his hand to flip the light switch just inside her cabin door. Surely he would not be joining them in the field she thought.

"I thought we would have breakfast together once we reach Roslyn. I have phoned ahead and Heath should have everything ready for us when we arrive. Can you be ready to go within the next 30 minutes?"

"By Heath I suppose you mean Dr. Heath Conrad." Cordie said without thinking. Her tone revealed the reluctance she felt about having to see Heath Conrad again. "Oh, please pardon me Felix. I don't suppose you know that the good Dr. Conrad and I have somewhat of a past together. And I use the term good derogatorily."

Felix walked further into her cabin and smiled warmly at the troubled Cordie. "I assure you Cordielia Emrys, there is very little about you that I am not aware of. I don't make it a practice of tracking down people for my projects without knowing as much as humanly possible about those people."

"No of course not." Cordie said sheepishly.

"We have an incredible job before us Cordie." Felix continued in a fatherly manner. "I know that your past with Heath may cause you some degree of agitation and believe me young lady, Heath Conrad can push nearly anyone's buttons. Still, he is a major part of this team and I know you will be able to handle him. All I ask is that you keep in mind the importance of what we are on the threshold of uncovering and leave Heath to me. I will keep him in line. Now, take a change of clothing and what ever else you will need for an overnight stay in Roslyn and let's get this adventure underway."

Felix's words did a great deal in calming Cordie, but she still wasn't any too eager to join up with her old acquaintance, Dr. Heath Conrad. Felix patted her small soft hand with his aged one and turned to leave her cabin.

"Thank you Felix." Cordie said to his back. "Thank you for including me in this and thank you Felix for not making me explain my past with Heath."

The old man turned to look over his shoulder and smiled at Cordie as he left her cabin. She dropped back down on the bed and closed her eyes tightly. No she really wasn't looking forward to standing face to face with Heath Conrad again.

Only a few minutes later, Cordie was ready to join the rest of the group. She had pulled her hair back in a tight braid, the way she had worn it nearly every time she had been with him. Her kaki shorts were loose fitting but shorter than she normally wore anymore and her soft blue t-shirt seemed to reflect the sparkling torques blue of her eyes. She may be older than he remembered but she would be dammed if she weren't going to look her best the first time he saw her after nearly 10 years.

Adam couldn't believe his eyes. Where had his ultra conservative, mild mannered co-professor gone and whom was this vibrant, and very attractive woman coming off the plane in her place. He had always though of Cordie as a nice looking, older woman, but he was seeing her in a whole new light this morning.

Bruce patted Adam on the back and said just loud enough for him to hear, "I wouldn't have minded working the last six years with our Dr. Emrys."

Adam could feel himself blush just a bit even though he had already come to feel comfortable with Bruce's easy manner of jesting. He respected Cordie and thought of her as a dear friend and colleague, but he had never really though of her in any kind of sexual context and after all she was nearly 15 years his senior. Not that anyone would have recognized as much the way she looked this morning.

"We need to make a very quick stop in Edinburgh, then on south just a few miles past the village of Roslyn. Rooms will be available for us in the castle of the Sinclair Family near Roslyn Chapel for the evening." Felix called out eagerly as Cordie joined the group ready to begin the drive.

Once comfortable inside the car, Cordie fell fast asleep. She realized it had been a mistake not to have gotten more rest on the plane last night and consciously decided that the drive would be her best chance to remedy that mistake.

Soon after allowing herself to fall into a comfortable sleep, Cordie began to see familiar images in her dreams. She was so young, yet she had learned so much from her schooling and work on similar field expeditions for the Vatican. Cordie had been sent to Labaantum to investigate the famous Crystal Skull known as the Skull of Doom that had been found there in 1927.

The church was sure that the rock crystal skull was authentic; it just wasn't sure that it had legitimately been found in Labaantum. Cordie had just left the laboratory of the Hewlett-Packard Company. She had gone to personally talk with the scientists who had done laser-beam tests a few years prior. Hewlett-Packard was a modern manufacturer of crystal oscillators and experts that Cordie knew she could trust. They had verified for her their conclusion that the skull had been manufactured from a single large crystal and polished for over 300 years to achieve the peculiar optical qualities it possessed. It was almost as if lenses had been inserted inside crystal.

One of the local priests had just finished sharing their ancient Maya ancestral myths with Cordie. They were making their way to the ruins of the Mayan temple where the skull had been found when a tall dark haired man suddenly appeared from behind the fallen stones of one of the smaller pyramids. The sun was beating down on his bear chest and the sweat on his perfectly tanned skin seemed to sparkle like tiny diamonds across his broad shoulders.

She should have turned and ran right them. Instead in her dream she remembered only the excitement of the next three weeks as she got to know the charming young man she only knew as Heath. He had acted like a school boy in love, given her wild flowers, taken her to dinner and telling her how lovely and completely enchanting she was. How could she have refused him when he asked her to join him on his exploration to find a lost city in the jungles of Brazil?

The Brazilian jungle, green lush and brimming with life, had been like nothing she had ever experienced before and she was experiencing it with a man that seemed totally committed to her. They slept, ate and explored together for another seven to eight weeks. She remembered standing one morning as the sun was just breaking through the mountains beside a wide river. Heath had caught them fresh fish for breakfast and she was gazing off into the green fields filled with flowers on the far side of the river. As the orange and pink hues came up over the mountain range Heath came up slowly behind her and wrapped his arms around her. She felt as if the whole world had vanished, time had stood still just for the two of them. There was nothing at that moment other than her and Heath and the waking wild flowers dancing to the sunrise across the wide river.

Adam flipped through the pages of the AA road map of the British Isles that Bruce had handed him and Bruce drove. Felix set in the back with Cordie and thought her idea to nap a bit on the way was as good an idea as any other. Before long he was sleeping comfortably as well. It gave Bruce and Adam a chance to talk casually and get to know each other a little better.

Being young single men, it didn't take long for the conversation to turn to the topic of young single women. Bruce talked about a few of the women he had dated at college but there didn't seem to be anyone that he had really missed since moving back to the Legacy House in Cairo last fall with his grandfather. Listening to Bruce caused Adam to recall for the first time since this adventure had begun, the incredible opportunity he was going to miss by not being at the university to teach the lovely young woman he had met yesterday. The recollection caused him to let out a stifled whimper like noise.

Bruce laughed as he asked, "What was that?"

"Oh nothing really, you wouldn't believe me if I told you. It would just sound like one of those stories guys tell other guys to make themselves look good." Adam replied dejectedly.

"Oh now then, let's hear it. Now you have to tell me." Bruce insisted.

"It really is nothing. It is just that after Cordie did her initial class introduction yesterday, the most beautiful dark haired goddess in the entire world approached me. She was concerned about some class time she might have to miss and of course I came to her rescue by assuring her I would work it all out with Dr. Emrys. I was so looking forward to seeing that lovely creature in class every day for the whole term, then I up and skip town." Adam replied

Both of the young men laughed at the story and Bruce made a minor attempt to make Adam feel better about the situation by telling him that he would put a good word in with his sister on Adam's behalf when she met up with them in Egypt later on.

CHAPTER 5

Roslyn Chapel complex built by William Sinclair in the mid-fifteenth century.

Cordie could have easily continued to sleep had she not felt the motion of the car stop. Unlike the brief stop they had made only a short while back in Edinburgh, when the car stopped this time, Bruce turned off the engine. Maybe it had been the sound of both the front doors of the car shutting, more so than the car stopping that had actually awaken her. All of the wonderful memories of those first few months with Heath had vanished and the cold hard reality of just how terrible it had all turned for them, as she got to know the real man, were again at the forefront of her mind. At any rate, Cordie was awake and realizing that she would have to see her old nemesis again face to face before long. She let out a slight sigh at the realization and began to ready herself mentally for what she knew would be at best still an awkward event.

"It won't be all that bad my dear." Felix said as if he could read her thoughts. "Now come along, lets join the young men before they get too far ahead of us."

Before Cordie could reach up to open the door of the car, it swung open from the effort of someone on the outside. To her total amazement a very polite, Heath Conrad bent down and stuck his face into the back of the car. "Let me help you out Cordie. It has been so long and I have so much to share with you." He said warmly as he extended his hand to help her out of the car.

Cordie was speechless at his warmth and what seemed to be genius enthusiasm in greeting her. After remembering the harsh words he had last spoken to her all those years ago, she wondered if this in fact could possibly be the same man she had left standing in a South American jail cell. Without really knowing it, she put her hand in his and allowed him to assist her.

His hand was large and strong just as she had remembered. At one point in time she had changed the entire direction of her life because of how the touch of that very hand had made her feel. Could he possibly have forgotten all that had come between them?

"There isn't anyone in all of the world that I would rather share this with Cordielia Emrys. I feel like a kid again. Wait until you see what we have uncovered!" Heath went on with a truly warm and sincere tone in his strong deep voice.

Adam had taken both his and Cordie's overnight bags from the trunk of the car and come up along side where Heath and Cordie stood. He didn't even seem to notice that Heath still held Cordie's small pale hand in his much larger much tanner one. "Well Dr. Conrad, if we are only here for the one night as planned then we have no time to waste standing around, now do we." Adam said sharply.

"Very good point Adam. Let me introduce you properly." Cordie said as she uncomfortably pulled her hand from his and backed a step further from Heath. "Dr. Heath Conrad it is my pleasure to introduce to you my teaching partner, and one of the sharpest linguistic minds I have every had the pleasure of working with, and my dear friend, Dr. Adam Khalid. And Dr. Khalid this is the well-known Dr. Heath Conrad. Now that the formalities are out of the way I think a first name basis should be more than adequate considering the circumstances."

Adam set down the bag in his right hand and extended it to Heath. The older man seemed to look at him as if he was sizing him up before returning the handshake. Both men had a firm grip, but Heath seemed not to have his heart in becoming acquainted with young Adam. He quickly turned all of his attentions back to Cordie and resumed speaking.

"I have everything set up in the dinning room so that I can bring you up to speed over breakfast. Felix thought that would be best, but then I want to get you down into the caves as soon as possible."

"Caves, I don't have the slightest idea why we are even in Scotland, let alone anything about any caves." Cordie responded.

"Well, that is what I am about to explain to you." Heath smiled and said with far too much charm to suit Adam.

The castle at Roslyn was not nearly as grand as the Legacy House castle further north in Fife. Still it was large enough to house the remaining decendent line of the Sinclair family in the main wing and still have ample guest accommodations. Breakfast had been set up in the formal dinning room just off the grand hall used for larger gatherings. Lovely 16th century tapestries covered the tall stonewalls with only the openings of the row of three large windows on the north side exposed.

At one end of the long dinning table a huge pull down screen had been set up. It was all that Heath could manage, to even allow everyone to be seated and have their plates served before he dimmed the lighting and began his presentation.

The first slide to appear on the screen was of a very ancient text inscribed with a language that even Adam could not place. "This is the solution, or at least a part of the solution. The problem is that no one alive today can read it." Heath said very dryly. "He looked down and across the table at Adam and added, "Unless of course our young linguistic genius knows something that the rest of the world population has forgotten."

Felix cleared his throat and without further action necessary Heath went on in a less argumentative manner. "As everyone in this room knows, Cordelia, our host and sponsor, Felix and myself have spent a great deal of our lives trying to piece together a more complete history of humankind. We are all in agreement that clues have been left all around this world of ours by some previously unidentified source. Clues, which suggest there has been highly, developed civilizations on this planet from a far far earlier time than traditional science would have us believe." Heath paused only slightly before he added confidently, "Well folks, we are on the verge of actually putting those clues together and solving the mystery of all time. The mystery of our most ancient ancestors and the civilization that they had developed."

Bruce looked puzzled as he watched his grandfather's face beam with satisfaction. He knew that there were many aspects of the Legacy House that he had not been schooled on, but he still thought that he knew enough about his grandfather to know he wouldn't allow himself to be taken in by someone as reckless with his claims as Heath Conrad. To see the confidence on his grandfather's face only led Bruce to believe that what Heath was saying was not an over exaggeration. Adam on the other hand had already taken an immediate dislike to the man and could not seem to get past his reputation. He set watching Heath as if he was ready to pounce on the first mistake he might make.

It was Cordie who was objective enough at the moment to ask, "What is it that we do know about the engraving in the slide that we are currently looking at?"

"We know that it was found in Egypt. We know from carbon dating that it is older than anything we have ever attempted to translate previously. And we know that it has something to do with revealing the secrets of The Lost Knowledge (Gnostic) therefore possibly The Lost Acquaintance." Heath replied without missing a beat. He was prepared and eager for a scientific challenge. He knew very well what he had and just how much there still was to achieve in order to know what "what they had" meant.

"Where in Egypt?" Cordie volleyed back at Heath

Heath shot Felix a disturbed look. For the first time in a very long time, Cordie knew she had caught Heath in a less than honest moment. She knew the look in his eye when he wanted to lie and it infuriated her that he had not changed. So much for the initial charm of Heath Conrad.

It was Felix's comforting voice that pulled her back to the present situation as he said, "That is not a relevant part of the issue at this point in time. I take responsibility for the possession of the piece. Let us simply accept that through Legacy House knowledge finding the piece has led us here to Roslyn. Now Heath, won't you please move on with why we are here and what Roslyn holds for us in terms of our mystery."

Adam had not moved. He was still staring intensely at the slide. Almost while Felix was still talking he allowed his thoughts to escape his lips without even realizing it. "Rudimentary mnemonic devices, prior even to cuneiform."

"What Adam, what are you seeing?" Felix asked immediately.

"Oh pardon me, I didn't realize I was actually speaking." Adam replied somewhat sheepishly. Of all of the times that he could have allowed his unchecked thoughts to be heard, why would it have had to be now in a room full of people he would have much rather impressed with some well thought out comments. "I am sorry. I was just observing the spacing and type of marking. I am sure that I haven't come up with anything that you didn't already know." He continued trying to save at least a little bit of his pride.

"No wait son." Felix said enthusiastically. "It is an obvious conclusion but we had not looked at it as a type of Proto-Writing system. We have been looking for the similar elements to the logographic language systems, wanting to put it all together to completely lay out what it says." Felix excitedly turned to Heath, "Don't you agree, this puts a whole new focus on trying to decipher the messages now doesn't it."

Heath changed the slide immediately. Adam was completely unaf-fected by Heath's actions. He had already taken a notepad from his pants pocket and started scribbling ideas in it.

Heath's next slide was of some sort of waterfall with lush green growth all around it. It puzzled Cordie that it was not a site that she was in anyway familiar with. She thought she knew pretty much every major archeological site in the world, if not from personal experience, than at least from photos. This was not a place she could ever recall hav-ing seen or studied.

"This is a waterfall which covers a cave entrance not 3 miles from here. What you most likely know of Roslyn is the suggested Templar association and the marvels of the medieval structure known as Roslyn Chapel. Adam, Denise and Felix will spend their time primarily in the Chapel, as I am sure it still holds many answers for us as well. However, it is here, to this waterfall that Bruce, Cordie and I will continue our parts of this expedition."

"Excuse me, but who is Denise?" Felix asked respectfully.

"Denise Jorgenson is the assistant that I spoke to you about Felix." Heath stopped to explain. "She will be joining us after breakfast. She has heard all of this more times than she cares to count and wanted to make sure her equipment was ready."

"And if it is not being too inquisitive Heath, could you share with us what Ms. Jorgenson's area of specialty is and what equipment she is checking?" Felix went on to inquire.

"Denise is a photojournalist. She will be photographing the engrav-ings and carvings within the chapel so that we might refer back to them if needed as our journey proceeds." Heath explained quickly then went on with his original explanation.

"It has been claimed that it was the Templars who found a great treasure burred under the ruins of King Solomon's Temple in Jerusalem. Although claiming to be a Christian order the Templars fell out of favor with the Pope and were persecuted and thought destroyed.

In an effort to make a long story a bit shorter, the treasure that was never recovered was believed by some to have secretly been transported here and hidden again within Roslyn Chapel or some said in underground passages or vaults. It has been suggested that Roslyn Chapel complex was a deliberate replication of the underground chambers of King Solomon's Temple. It is my belief now that Roslyn Chapel complex is in fact of deliberate replication, but of something much much older and more significant than anything that could have been buried under Solomon's Temple. Or that at the very least Solomon's Temple was also a replication of that same much older site and the information found there was then reproduced again here for protection and to maintain the secret knowledge it represented."

Adam, who had only recently stopped scribbling in his notepad, was still stuck back on the photojournalist part of Heath's revelations. He supposed that at least now, he did not have to feel like the lightest member of the team. After all, even a linguist and junior professor should surely rank higher on the ladder than a photojournalist.

Bruce shifted in his chair nearly at the same point as Adam had and then their attention was drawn to Cordie. "You have found something significant under the chapel then?" she asked.

"I would defiantly say so!" Heath regained his enthusiasm as he spoke directly to Cordie. "I believe that what I am about to show you is an exact duplication of an original storage place of three very important keys. Keys that have rested quietly under a great marker for longer than most people believe humans have existed on this earth of ours."

"What good is a duplicate, why aren't we going after the keys themselves?" Adam said before he could stop himself. Again he had not intended to say anything out loud and he was sorry he had even before the words had finished leaving his mouth.

To everyone's surprise, instead of Heath responding with irritation, he simply replied without taking his eyes off Cordie. "Well, that is exactly what we are going to do, and won't it be a much simpler task having gotten a feel for the layout of things ahead of time."

It was at that point that Felix placed his napkin on his finished breakfast plate and stood. He patted his grandson on the shoulder as he walked past him and headed toward the end of the table where Heath stood. "I am going to expedite things a bit at this point, if there are no objections."

Heath finally turned his focus from Cordie and took a seat in the chair nearest where he and Felix now stood. Felix straightened his vest, stood up a bit straighter and began where Heath had left off.

"We do not have all the pieces of the puzzle as of yet, but we are assuredly much closer to collecting them all than anyone could imagine. From the writings that we have found, the links found here at Roslyn and what we hope to find in Cairo and then in our final destination, located somewhere in Central or South America, we think we will be able to prove that the materials we have found are the source documents used in much of the most ancient mysteries of our history. We are sure it was from this source that some of the earliest maps of our planet were drawn. It is not at all a far reach to believe that this discovery is going to answer the questions that have baffled humankind in relationship to the creation of our universe, the knowledge of all humankind and how such information and knowledge was lost to us. As Heath and I have discussed and come to complete agreement and understanding on, the only way that we are going to be successful in our endeavor is to work as a team. Each of us has something significant to contribute to this project, even if we are not all completely in agreement as to exactly what it is that each of us is contributing at all times or the worth of that contribution. I must insist that as we leave this room this morning and begin our work, each of you agree that we are all, all 8 of us in this until the end and that we will put what ever unproductive feelings that we may have or that may arise aside until after we have accomplished our goal."

Adam knew that Felix was including his granddaughter, the young man to join them in Egypt and Heath's assistant Denise when he totaled the group to account for a total of 8 individuals. At the present with only five of them in the large dinning room, it was already beginning to feel somewhat cramped. He couldn't help it. It didn't matter whether this Heath Conrad was a genius or not, he didn't like him. He had not expected to like him, but he had also not expected to dislike him so completely. He didn't know whether it was the way the man addressed him personally, the way he referred to Cordie as Cordielia or simply the way he looked at her. What ever it was, Adam knew he was going to have to be very careful not to show his dislike for Heath. As for the rest of the group, how bad could a female photojournalist and an heiress to The Legacy House be? If Bruce's sister was anything like her brother, she certainly wouldn't be a problem. So the only other person to be concerned with would be Felix's Egyptian astronomer.

Bruce knew he could get along with anyone but he set quietly to see what kind of reaction the rest of the group was going to have on his grandfather speech. It was Cordie who spoke up after the moments of silence following what Felix had said. Her voice didn't have the same demure quality that Adam had come to find so comforting. Instead she spoke with a bit of apprehension and a somewhat weak quality circling about her words. "I am sure you know what you are talking about Felix. We are all here because we do have something to contribute and that is exactly what we each need to focus on. Now what is it that we should be doing now that our breakfast has been finished?"

"Just what I wanted to hear." Felix added, "Bruce you can help Cordie get settled in and join Heath down by the south entrance. He will take you down to the falls. Adam why don't you and I try to find this Denise and get started inside the chapel. We can finish this background presentation at any time, let's get on to the current work at hand."

CHAPTER 6

Standing outside the chapel Adam couldn't believe how run down and even dilapidated the building looked. It certainly didn't give him the impression of anything out of the ordinary for the remains of a medieval stone structure. The mid morning Scottish sky was gray and full of blotches of almost black clouds, which Adam hoped, wouldn't burst loose with rain anytime soon. Maybe it was the gray of the morning along with his reservations about Heath that were causing him to have such a gloomy impression of this chapel that Felix seemed to feel was so important.

"Wait until you see the inside." A friendly energetic voice sprang up from behind.

Adam turned and saw Denise. She was nearly six foot tall, very athletically built, sharp but feminine and with a smile that should probably be in front of, instead of behind the cameras she had hanging over both shoulders. And she was very young looking, with the flawless skin found only in the still very young. Her face and body were upstaged only by the tumultuous mass of flowing dark hair, which fell freely down her back.

"You must be our photojournalist." Adam replied with as much enthusiasm as his present mood would allow.

"I guess your right, that would be me, Denise Jorgenson with cameras in hand." Denise continued as she walked on past Adam and led the way toward the chapel entrance. "Have you been inside yet? You just aren't going to believe this place."

It almost seemed to Adam that the cloud cover of the gray morning began to break just as Denise pushed open the large door. The slightly broken cloud coverage instantly allowed the sun to release its rays to dance dramatically on the multitude of pinnacles of the chapel.

Felix has already entered the chapel as Denise motioned for Adam to join them. Felix had gone ahead through the nave and toward the free-standing pillars farther into the chapel. Denise waited for Adam; she wanted to see the look on his face when he saw the tapestry of images carved into stone. It was almost a dizzying effect to try to take it all in at once the first time you saw the massive imagery built into Roslyn.

Adam didn't disappoint Denise. His face almost instantly revealed the amazement he was feeling as his eyes bounced from the disorientation of pagan, Islamic, Egyptian, Celtic, Jewish, Templar and even Masonic imagery. She allowed him a few minutes of private contemplation of what his eyes were saying to his mind before she laughed softly and took his arm to lead him toward the carving of the maize along one of the arches. She had already photographed both the arch of American maize plants and the wall containing the carvings of the Aloe plants that proved a knowledge of the Americas long before Columbus had set sail for the New World, but she knew he would want to see them for himself.

By the time Felix finished examining the Apprentice Pillar and its four floral swaths he found Adam and Denise setting on a pew looking down at the thick stone flooring. There was something about the way the swaths spiraled down and around the fluted center of the corners of the top to meet the base at its opposite side that Felix knew meant something. He just couldn't put his finger on it and he knew it was something that should mean something significant to him.

"Adam, I have something that I would like you to look at son." Felix's troubled voice broke the silence of the chapel. "Maybe you will come across something in the language databases that will shed some light on this. You don't mind, do you Denise?"

"Oh not at all Mr. Smith." Denise said quite formally as she jumped to a standing position. "We have not be introduced but I am Denise Jorgensen and very pleased to be included in on this expedition."

Felix shook loose from his troubled thoughts and looked at the lovely young woman. "Felix, please. Yes Heath did tell me about your inclusion in our little group here. Welcome aboard young lady."

Denise let out a slight breath of relief that Felix did not seem to be against her being a part of the team. Heath had explained that Felix Smith was the most important person on this project. She had known Heath Conrad for several years and she had never known him to yield authority or control to anyone before. She didn't know exactly what it was that Felix had on Heath, but what ever it was, Heath was certainly not going to get out of line or do anything to get onto Felix's bad side. He had made it perfectly clear to Denise that if their plan was to work, she would have to ingratiate herself with Felix Smith.

She would agree to take the photos and document the steps of their journey just as Heath had instructed her to. Felix would go along with it as long as she agreed that nothing was to be published until it had been cleared by The Legacy House. Still, if even a small part of what Heath suggested was to be found on this expedition, Denise Jorgensen knew that her coverage as Dr. Heath Conrad's private biographer would land her the next Nobel Prize. That was what she was thinking about as Felix and Adam left her standing by the pew to go back and take another look at the right hand pillar that had Felix so troubled. Had his mind not been so preoccupied with what ever it was he couldn't put his finger on, he may have seen through Denise right away? After all, Felix Smith had not gotten where he was in life without being able to read people pretty well.

It was still difficult for Cordie not to allow her personal feelings and memories of the time she and Heath had spent together, to get in the way of the work ahead of them. It had been a short drive from the castle down along a village path to the waterfall, but she hadn't said hardly a word. Bruce did a wonderful job of keeping Heath's attention off of her, by asking all kinds of questions about the rock structure and geological make up of the underground chambers.

"Cordielia, have you kept in shape for your climbing?" Heath asked as he pulled ropes and equipment out of the car trunk.

"Don't I look like I've stayed in shape!" Cordie flung back at Heath before thinking about her response.

Heath smiled that devilish smile that she remembered all too well and said over his shoulder to Bruce, "Guess that wasn't the best of questions to asked right off the bat."

It infuriated Cordie that he could get to her so easily and what was worse was that she hadn't climbed anything more difficult than a flight or two of stairs at the university in years. On the other hand, it was obviously apparent that Heath had maintained his roughed lifestyle. He might have aged and have bits of gray showing through his otherwise dark curls right around his temple area, but beyond that, he looked just as well built and capable as he had been the last time she had seen him. Of course the last time she had seen him, he was standing behind the bars of a grimy South American jail without a shirt. His chest was nearly hairless and gleaming with sweat from the struggle he had put up against the men who had dragged him from a local military officers home. It had been the last straw in their turbulent relationship. He had paid far too much attention to the daughter of the military officer and had been caught after sneaking into her bedchamber.

Cordie could not stop the flow of memories no matter how desperately she wanted to. She could even smell the ranched cigar smoke of the jailer as he stood behind her when she had been taken into see Heath. He had tried to tell her that it was all a mistake and that he was just using the girl to get information on a local pyramid location. He knew that if he could locate the fabled pyramid he would find a golden and turquoise mask that he had already spent nearly six months digging for.

They had been arguing for weeks about Heath's intention to steal the mask once he found it. Nuns in a strict Catholic monetary had raised Cordie to believe in the importance of truth and not violating the rights of others. Heath continued to tell her that she was just sheltered and naïve, not understanding the ways of the real world. She had almost come to a point of believing him until he had pushed it just too far. To steal a relic form a poor South American village that would have benefited greatly by the discovery of such a mask was something that she just couldn't justify. She never had really convinced herself whether she had finally left Heath because of his dishonest business dealings or his unfaithfulness in using that young girl.

At any rate, that was the last time Cordie had seen Heath. That hot stifling day standing with those dirty rusted bars between them as she turned and left him standing there and headed straight back to the United States. She knew that if she had paid the jailer, he would have released Heath. She chose not to and left him there to rot for all she cared. Now here she was standing not four feet from him again. Something she had promised herself she would never let happen.

"I am sure we will all make the climb just fine." Bruce announced casually in an effort to move things along.

"Of course we will." Heath added. "Behind the falls is a cave about 80 feet long. Near the far end is an incredible man made entrance that we will have to lower each other through to reach the labyrinth below. It is truly amazing the amount of man made tunneling and construction that has been accomplished under the chapel foundation. There are stairs and tunnels that lead no where at all and if you do not know exactly what you are doing you could be lost in the labyrinth forever."

"Well aren't we lucky then that we are being led by someone who always knows exactly what he is doing." Cordie said with a bite.

The three moved easily enough through the somewhat slippery rock cover of the waterfall base and back into the cave. The cave its self was nothing out of the ordinary for the area and it didn't surprise Bruce at all that no one had seen the need to further explore it previously.

It wasn't until they had all three been lowered down into the truly amazing and complexly constructed labyrinth below the cave that Bruce or Cordie really began to feel the excitement of what they were about to begin. It was incredible. The tunnels were perfectly smooth and shaped with a geometrical accuracy that neither had seen beneath ground before. They both followed Heath attached to each other by a short lead rope for safety. It seemed to Bruce that they had gone down at least three separate flights of stairs not to mention any decline that was sloped into the tunnels. There were literally miles upon miles of varying tunnel options that they could have taken, but Heath did not hesitate at any turn. He knew exactly where he was headed. Bruce couldn't understand how the fresh air was being circulated so deep within the earth, but it was. The air was fresh and crisp, not at all stale or in any way lacking.

"Just around this next turn we are going to come upon a door. It is a solid stone door and until very recently, I do not think it had been opened for hundreds of years." Heath explained.

Just as he had said, they turned the corner and there stood a huge solid stone door. Bruce immediately recognized that the stone of the door was not at all the same as the stone in which the tunnels had been carved from. He couldn't be absolutely sure without tests, but he thought the stone was a type of Egyptian sand stone. But how would such a door have ever found its way from the quarries of Egypt to Scotland of all places?

Cordie and Bruce were still both holding their breath in anticipation when Heath pushed open the stone door. They all three stepped into the small empty room carved into the center of this mass of confusing tunnels.

"It is just an empty chamber?" Cordie said very softly in the form of a question more to herself than anyone else.

"Yes, you are right. It is just an empty chamber but if I am correct then it is not just an empty chamber in the original site. Remember this is just a duplicate. A map of what to expect so to speak." Heath tried to explain in a very convincing manner. "You see it isn't what is in this chamber that is important. It is that we have found the chamber and have mapped it out so that when we are underground at the original location we will be able to find this same chamber."

"We want to find this same empty chamber at another site?" Bruce asked inquisitively and with a little apprehension in his tone.

"Okay, it may not all make perfectly good sense to you now, but believe me it will. Once we have the rest of the translation of the map tablets we will know exactly what it is we are to find in the other chamber. This one, was just suppose to be a map to prepare us for finding the original chamber once we get into the original labyrinth." Heath replied in an almost pleading form of an explanation.

Bruce was back to studying the strange stone door and Cordie wasn't really sure what to make of the empty chamber. There wasn't the first bit of archeological information to be found. It was strangely barren of any clues to culture or time. Heath's theory that it was a deliberate copy or practice map of some kind was beginning to sound like a real possibility to Cordie.

For the next several hours Heath led Cordie and Bruce in and out of the inner chamber in an effort to familiarize them both with the passageways. Bruce continued to do a wonderful job of not allowing Cordie to be left alone for any length of time with Heath. After several hours of climbing, crawling and exploring Cordie had almost forgotten her apprehension about being around Heath again. Nether said or did anything to bring back the memory of their turbulent past.

CHAPTER 7

The dinner buffet was set up on the sidebar in the dinning room. At the far end of the long formal table, two computer terminals had been set up near the pull down screen Heath had used that morning. Adam was already at work at the terminal on the left. He knew that if he could just figure out a few more elements of the obscure language used in the tablets he would be able to break the code. He had seen many clues in Roslyn Chapel, but nothing that was clear in the way of explaining the tablets.

Denise was already filling her plate with steamed vegetables and fresh fruit. Her long hair was hanging loosely down her back nearly down to her long tan legs. Bruce couldn't help but stop and take a second look as he entered the dinning room. Adam was too involved to notice but Felix smiled and shook his head at his young grandson's reaction.

"Come in Bruce." Felix said to break the silence. "I am glad to see that Heath didn't allow you to get lost down in his tunnels. What did you think of Heath's expedition today?"

Denise turned to the sound of Felix's voice. She was anxious to meet Bruce as well. Heath had told her as much as he could about each of the members of the group, but he really hadn't had all that much to say about Bruce.

"It wouldn't have been too difficult to get lost down there. Have you been down and seen those pathways grandfather?" Bruce replied.

"No I have saved what energy I may need to use in climbing for the final destination." Felix admitted. "You know, your old grandfather isn't nearly as young as the rest of this group. Speaking of young, let me do the honors of introducing you to the lovely young Denise Jorgensen."

Denise had already set her plate down and had begun to move toward Bruce with her hand extended. "It is a pleasure to meet another member of the Smith family. Your grandfather has impressed me greatly today with his knowledge of the symbolism depicted within the stonework of the chapel. I understand that he has passed all of his wealth of knowledge on to you and your sister."

"Well, that I don't know is true, but I am happy to meet you as well." Bruce said as he took the bold young woman's hand and shook it firmly. She was definitely a charmer and a looker to boot. "I am sorry that we didn't have an opportunity to meet earlier today, but Heath was quite anxious to show us his discovery."

"Well, that is Heath for you, always wanting to show off his discoveries." Denise jested with a smile.

"Adam, what is keeping you so intently occupied down there that you aren't even interested in joining us at this end of the room?" Bruce asked changing his attention from Denise momentarily. "I see Denise has already filled her plate. Should we join her?"

Adam eventually did look up in response but Bruce had already helped Denise to her seat and moved over to the sidebar to begin filling his own plate. Unlike the dainty little helpings that Denise had taken, Bruce was filling his plate with a large helping of steaming hot roast beef, potatoes and gravy. Evidently his day of exploring the tunnels beneath Roslyn Chapel had allowed him to work up quite an appetite.

"Yes, come on Adam you need to eat. I asked for the buffet setting so that we could continue to work while eating, but you do need to at least fill a plate and make an attempt to take in some nourishment." Felix added as he slowly moved toward the sidebar as well.

There was something about Felix that just instilled confidence and a desire to follow his instructions. As much as Adam wanted to continue his work, he did as Felix had told him and stood. Then just as he was about to move away from the computer terminal it hit him. The key he had been searching for was right in front of him. How could he have not seen it from the beginning! He let out a crisp loud, "Yes" and bent back down over the keyboard. He didn't even take the time to set back down. He just squatted down and began pecking on the keyboard frantically.

"What is it boy? What have you found?" Felix said with enthusiasm. "Do you have something?"

Within seconds Felix, Bruce and Denise were all standing behind Adam watching his computer screen with anticipation. The excitement was growing and Adam couldn't even speak for thinking to himself and pecking away at the keyboard.

Felix saw the movement of the characters on the screen and understood before either of the others what Adam had discovered. He was right from the beginning, it wasn't a language in the sense of words being written, as someone would have spoken them. No it was just as Adam had initially thought it was simply scattered pieces of information to be used as keys to shake the memory of the storyteller.

"Look here Felix." Adam said frantically as he pointed at the screen. "This right here is talking about a time before the flood: the First time and the creation of a material universe in the image of the spiritual universe. Here, do you see it?"

"Yes Adam, yes I do. You have done it. This is a form of writing older than any Aramaic or Hieroglyphics we have ever found, and you are the man who has deciphered it. What is this right here?" Felix said as he pointed to a lower character further to the left of the second row of the tablet.

"I'm not totally sure yet, but I think it is referring to a man and his son's. Maybe it is En… Enoch, that's it the man's name is Enoch." Adam said slowly.

"Enoch, well done son!" Felix patted Adam on the back and reached out to grasp the arm of Bruce. "Enoch and the book of Enoch can tell us much."

Just that moment Cordie and Heath came in the main door together. They had been talking together about something and were nearly in the dinning room before they realized that something significant was going on at the other end of the table.

"Yes, Enoch. Come in Cordie and tell us what you can about Enoch." Felix continued with delight.

Everyone looked up and waited breathlessly for Cordie to respond. She looked puzzled, gave Heath a quick glance and then slowly began moving toward the group as she spoke.

"Well, Enoch was the seventh pre-flood patriarch in the Bible. Enoch is identified as that son of man who functions as the eschatological judge, a judge who reverses the fortunes of his oppressed people and of their oppressors who are termed "the kings and the mighty" In the lost books of Enoch there are detailed accounts of angels, called Watchers, who are involved with showing Enoch much of the earth and heaven. He taught a solar calendar and received revelations about the future through mantic means such as symbolic dreams. But I am sure that you would have already know all of that Felix, what does Enoch have to do with the tablets?"

"We aren't completely sure just yet, but come look at what Adam has done so far dear." Felix replied.

"O okay, look at this symbol I think it is a representation for leader, see how it is repeated here and again down here." Adam interjected as he pointed to the screen.

Cordie moved in closer and leaned down over Adam. She rested her right arm on his left shoulder and began studying the screen. "Is there any mention of a Shemihazah or Saklas? I'm looking for any reference to talk of any authentic truths of existence."

"Not that I have discovered yet, but let's look down here a little further." Adam replied with excitement.

Heath stood a few steps away from the group watching Cordie in her easy familiar manner with Adam. He had not expected to see Cordie and Adam on such familiar terms nor had he expected to feel anything towards Cordie. With all his faults, the one thing that Heath knew and understood very well was himself and his own motivations. He was in this for the fame and riches, definitely not for the girl. Why should it irritate him so to see Cordelia Emrys leaning up so closely to some young upstart academic?

He shook his head as if to clear his own thoughts, trying to refocus his attentions and interest on the information that Adam was revealing rather than how close he and Cordie appeared. It didn't help. The next thing he realized Heath found himself back in South America watching Cordie walking away from him. She was wearing one of his long white cotton shirts and walking from the bed toward the curtain separating the bedchamber and the bathroom of their small apartment.

"Well, don't you think so Heath?" Felix's voice shattered the fond memory of Heath's mind and pulled him back to the present.

"Oh, what was that Felix? I...I guess I wasn't listening." Heath stumbled in response.

Everyone turned their attention for the first time in nearly 30 minutes from Adam's computer screen to look up at Heath. There were only a few moments of silence before Heath made another attempt to recover. "The tablet isn't going to go anywhere, how about continuing the discussions over our dinner?"

Felix straightened up and joined Heath in encouraging everyone to take a break for the dinner meal. Bruce set the plate of cold roast beef he had already served himself aside and started filling a fresh plate. Denise set down at the place where her fruit and vegetables set and waited for the rest of the group to join her. Cordie and Adam were the last to fill their plates and be seated. It was apparent that Cordie was pleased and extremely excited about the breakthroughs that Adam had made. Heath on the other hand was still quite uncomfortable with his focus and attentions on Cordie and Adam. There was definitely too much on the line for him to be thinking about some sexual or emotional attachment he may have once felt toward Cordelia. After all, hadn't she left him behind bars in a South America?

CHAPTER 8

"Alright, lets recap what we have accomplished today." Felix began the conversation after everyone had been seated around the table with their full plates of roast beef, vegetables, potatoes, gravy and fresh baked bread.

"Could I take a try at it Felix?" Denise spoke up surprising both Felix and probably everyone in the room, with the possible exception of Heath who had secretly coached her very well. "If I am understanding everything thus far, Heath dug up a piece of an ancient pillar and procured three ancient clay tablets and several maps printed on strange rice paper like parchments near the Bahariya Oasis in Egypt. One of the clay tablets was a diagram that Cordie has easily verified as a type of map of the Nile valley. The second is the tablet that Adam has started deciphering that seems to be in some very ancient writing system that uses those wedge shapes to display ideas meant to remind a story teller of key elements of the tale he is passing on. So far we know that it is talking about a biblical figure, Enoch. And the third tablet was again a type of diagram or map showing three very different locations, one we believe is in Egypt but not necessarily around the Bahariya Oasis area, and the other two somewhere in Central or South America. The Egyptian location shows a treasure chamber with three crystals of some kind, which are clearly needed as keys to unlocking information at the second and possibly the third sites. From information Felix has access to through the Legacy House, we are here because we had reason to believe that clues had been left here as to how to find the first site in Egypt. How am I doing so far?" Denise paused like a child waiting for praise from Heath or Felix.

"Very well, I would say." Heath quickly praised, "You have very accurately summarized most of the key elements."

"Well, let me go on then." Denise said proudly and with a glowing smile. "The Legacy House is an ancient organization that has passed on certain bits of knowledge down through direct family lines from generation to generation. They have reason to believe that another group of "watchers" or guardians of some secretly guarded ancient knowledge, the Templars or Masons, built the complex here at Roslynn. Everyone knows that the Templars were the knights who dug under the ruins of King Solomon's temple in Jerusalem during the crusades. There has been much speculation as to what the treasure the Templars found really consisted of. What ever it was, it has been speculated also that it was eventually brought here to Scotland and secured away here within the Roslyn Chapel. Heath now believes that the treasure was the knowledge of the first site mentioned on the second tablet and that the underground chambers here are a duplicate of what will be found at the Egyptian site. So by finding the labyrinth below the chapel and mapping out the path to the inner chamber, Heath will be able to find the real inner chamber holding the keys once we are in the Egyptian site."

Cordie had not taken a single bit of the food on her plate. She didn't know exactly why but hearing this overly simplified explanation of the very remarkable finds, by this almost uneducated young child just appalled her. To reduce the significance of what they were involved in to a couple of unscientific paragraphs as she had was enough to cause her to loose her appetite. Instead, while everyone else seemed to be enjoying their dinner and listening contently to little miss photojournalist, Cordie was developing an intense dislike toward Denise.

"Well, I guess that is it in a nut shell." Felix concluded. "It seems that you have paid attention quite well. You do understand that none of this is for public consumption until after we have completed our mission." Felix added in a cautionary manner.

"Oh, of course Felix. Heath has been very clear that only upon approval from the Legacy House will I be allowed to publish anything of our expedition. I simply wanted to let all of you know that even though I am the youngest and only non-scientific member of the group, I do have a grasp of what is going on." Denise replied in a completely submissive and charming tone, which only served to aggravate Cordie even more so than she had already been.

"Cordelia you look as if you have something on your mind." Heath interjected softly.

"Oh, no nothing really; nothing other than contemplating what else your discoveries of the tablet might bring us. I am very anxious to get back to work on it, aren't you?" Cordie replied as she hoped desperately that Heath had not picked up on her reaction to Denise.

Felix stood slowly; he straightened his vest and paused for a moment prior to saying anything. "I think that I will turn in early this evening and leave the clues in the much younger and very capable hands of the rest of you. Bruce, if you wouldn't mind, I'd like to speak to you privately."

Bruce, who hadn't said a word all through dinner, shook his head and finished his last piece of roast beef. He stood and followed his grandfather out of the dinning room. Once Felix was sure they were out of voice range of anyone left in the dinning room, he put his arm around his grandson, patted his shoulder caringly and began, "Son, I know that you must have questions about what Denise said in there about the Legacy House."

"Well grandfather, I was a little taken back by her comments but I have always trusted that you tell me what I need to know." Bruce said with sincere trust in his voice.

"You are so like your father Bruce. It is almost like having him back with us when you are around son. You know, I really miss your old dad.

It seems so long ago that we lost he and your mother. I only thank God that I have had you and your dear sister so near all these years." Felix continues as they made their way into his bedchamber at the far end of that wing of the castle. "Here lets set near the window, there is a nice breeze and you can smell the Scottish thistles in the air this evening. There are things we need to talk of."

Bruce lovingly followed his grandfather over to the two large high backed chairs setting near the long full-length open window. He waited for Felix to be seated and then took the chair opposite him and waited quietly. Felix looked as if he was remembering something very pleasant and Bruce didn't want to interrupt his thoughts. He had loved his grandfather's gentle ways since he and his sister had moved into the Cairo Legacy House shortly after the death of their parents. Even during the terrible months following the accident, his grandfather had never raised his voice to either of the children. Bruce remembered his telling the servants that even though the young master and lady were merely 12 years old, their requests were to be honored just as his own.

"Bruce, I know that you think you know as much as you need to about the nature of our family and the Legacy House, but there is a great deal that you don't know. Your sister has been schooled in the responsibilities of becoming the Watcher after I am gone, but you have not been fully told of your heritage as one of the decedents of our line."

"You make it sound very mysterious grandfather." Bruce interrupted.

"That is quite an understatement son." Felix shook his head and smiled as he went on. "It is not that I have any doubts that your sister will do a fine job in her role, but the two of you are twins, born only minutes of each other. Maybe in such a case it would be acceptable for the two of you to share the family responsibilities."

A loud knock at the door interrupted Felix. It was quite strange that anyone would intrude on Felix once he had gone to his private bedchamber. Bruce turned in the direction of the door as the large brass knob began to turn slowly.

"I am sorry to interrupt," Cordie's voice sounded out excitedly as she poked her head into the slightly opened door. "Please forgive me, but I really think you would want to see what Adam has discovered!"

Felix looked at Bruce and indicated with a smile that their talk would have to wait. Both men stood and moved quickly to follow Cordie back to the dinning room.

Adam was beaming with satisfaction and even Heath seemed to be pleased with the young linguist. Heath had the slide of the tablet projected up on the large white screen and Adam was circling groupings of the wedge shaped writings.

"Felix, I really think that we have it. Look here," Adam nearly cried out as Cordie returned with Bruce and Felix. "It is a complex and distinctive myth of origin running through seven separate groupings of information. Just as we had started to discover before dinner, the first here talks about the keys or crystals and Enoch. But look down here it is laying out the importance of wisdom or Sophia and what was stolen from her. Then this third grouping is indicating something about the offspring, seed or posterity of Seth and indicates it equals the offspring of the light. I am not quite clear on this fourth grouping but it is referring to a prison or bondage but then it moves to destiny and the body. We still have some work in understanding this one. The fifth grouping here though is clearly talking about the island of seven caves, which seems to mean something very significant to Heath. I am still working on the sixth and seventh groupings."

Felix could not believe what he was hearing, but somehow he knew that every bit of it was correct. He could almost see it in the wedged markings as if they had transformed themselves into one of the languages he could read himself. Suddenly, he was beginning to wonder if perhaps Adam Khalid could not have also been a descendent of his own people. He knew that only someone with the acquaintance in his heart would have been able to make such quick discoveries that would all lead to supporting the mission of the Legacy House. Could this really be the information that generations of his family line had searched for?

CHAPTER 9

Cordie and Adam spent a great deal of the rest of the night pulling together all of the information they could on the current clues Adam had uncovered. Despite Cordie's dislike for Denise, they used her research and computer skills to locate and pull up the most reliable copies possible of the first and second books of Enoch.

Enoch was the grandson of Adam and the son of Cain. He was the father of Methuselah who was the grandfather of Noah. It had been Lamech the son of Methuselah whose wife bore a child, Noah. The baby Noah was born with pure white and rosy red skin, unlike the brown skin of his fathers. Enoch had been awaken one night by two shinning creatures. They transported him to a place full of light without any darkness, which was covered with snow and ice and was at the ends of the earth.

It was Bruce who was most interested in this portion of the Enoch tale. He worked for hours going back and forth over the information Denise was printing off. The passages telling of Enoch's transportation around the earth caused Bruce to remember that ancient Egyptian priests had used knotted cords to measure and plan their temples. Could the lost *Book of Enoch* be a detailed description of a very early geological survey taken of the earth?

'And I saw in those days how long cords were given to the Angels, and they took themselves wings and flew, and went towards the north. And

I asked an Angel, saying unto him: "Why have they taken cords and gone off?" and he replied: "They have gone to measure.'

In another portion of the Book of Enoch Bruce read over and over again, 'And these measures shall reveal all the secrets of the depths of the earth'

"Denise, can you find anything on Uriel or Uriel's Machines?" Bruce asked.

"Are you on to something Bruce?" Cordie asked excitedly.

"I think so, what do you know about the theories on a symmetrical grid of sacred latitudes possibly resulting from a ancient worldwide geographical knowledge of the surface of the earth?" Bruce replied

By now everyone except Denise, who was already working on finding the new information Bruce had asked for, had moved around Bruce. He was now looking at Chapter 65 of the Book of Enoch.

"I think this is indicating significant geological events taking place prior to the flood. And it would indicate that the shinning ones were able to use the measurements of the earth and their knowledge of the movements of the stars to somehow monitor the seismic movement of the earth. I wish Amehd were here. This really runs over into his area. I can handle the evidence of geology being an ancient science but I need Amehd for the astronomy and geometry."

"You're doing fine Bruce." Cordie reassured him. "Now how do these discoveries play with our belief that the Egyptian site is somehow connected to Giza and the Great Pyramid?"

Heath was sure the original site was somehow connected to Giza, but he didn't have the scientific evidence to prove it. Suddenly he was very attentive to what Bruce might be adding.

"Well, if we go back to the case Professor Charles Piazzi Smyth made in 1884 for the prime meridian of the world being made the north-south line that ran through the Great Pyramid and use that as our 0 degree longitude, it only makes since that we should find the first site in

Giza. Again this is more Amehd's area and it would really be better to wait until we are together in Egypt to try to go too much further."

It was getting late and everyone reluctantly agreed to wrap it up and try to get some sleep before heading out for the jet early in the morning. Only Denise stayed behind in the dinning room as the rest of the group left. She just wanted to check out a few more locations on the internet that might yield her some additional finds on Bruce's request for information. Heath had made it very clear to her that she needed to get as close to the others as possible. Their deception would only work if the others trusted her and the best way she knew to accomplish that was to become indispensable to them.

CHAPTER 10

Amehd stood in the delightful tranquility that could only be found in a few corners of Cairo, waiting anxiously for the jet to land. He could just barely still hear the familiar sound of the music of men in constant chanting efforts of praise to Allah. Like many Egyptian men, Amehd recognized and appreciated Cairo's inherent struggles between the allure of the ancient world and the necessities of a modern city. Only in Cairo was the subtle interweaving of the most ancient mystical and the modern mundane so apparent yet still alluring.

He could hardly wait to have everyone together to tell them that he had succeeded in making special arrangements to allow them access to the lower cavities leading to the underground treasures of the Sphinx. He had not been at all sure that he would be able to pull it off when Felix had told him what he needed Amehd to accomplish while he was gone. It was highly irregular and he knew that he would have to use unorthodox means to accomplish his goal. It was just that he had been raised in a very traditional Egyptian family and unorthodox was not within his natural way of handling things.

"Amehd, Amehd have they landed yet?" a familiar, yet totally unexpected voice sounded out from behind him.

Amehd turned quickly to see Mr. Smith's granddaughter running up toward the car. She and Bruce were twins, but Amehd knew that as much as Mr. Smith loved Bruce it was his special little granddaughter that held his heart in her hands. Having been born just minutes before Bruce she was also the one obligated to continue as a Watcher in the Legacy House.

"I missed you at the house Amehd. They told me you had brought the car to pick up grandfather and the team." She said as she reached her dear friend and grandfather's favorite apprentice in Egypt.

"My lady, what are you doing here? I understood that you were attending a class in the United States and could not be with us for several weeks." Amehd replied with his palms turned up and great surprise in the tone of his voice.

"Wait until you hear the story Amehd. Only in the States could such a scandal break out in a conservative Christian university. I thought I had made arrangements to begin the class and be allowed to miss the two weeks needed for the South American trip. Then when I showed up for class on day 2, the room was empty and there was a note taped to the door that everyone should see the registrar to withdraw and get into an alternative class before the deadline. I wasn't interested in any other class but I went down to the registrar's office to see what I could find out about the cancellation of the class. It seems that both the primary professor and her very handsome and charming young teaching assistant had both just left leaving nothing more than very uninformative letters of resignations and no explanations. The school officials were doing their best to play down the whole situation but the rumors were flying about the two of them running off to some tropical island together. You never would have known it to meet her, but I guess the professor had been a bit of a risk to begin with when the school hired her. I didn't stick around long enough to get all the details but I guess she came to the school nearly 10 years ago leaving behind some kind of scandal and had always been very reserved and conservative around the campus. It was quite the shocker that she would throw it all away to skip off to some tropical island paradise."

"Together maybe, but to a tropical island, I think not." The stern voice of her grandfather chimed in from behind her. "I assure you Gabriella that neither Dr. Emrys nor Dr. Khalid are off on any romantic excursion."

Gabriella twisted excitedly around to see her beloved grandfather and his team standing behind her. She through her arms around Felix's neck and laughed out loud as Cordie and Adam stood staring horrified at each other. Neither of them had even considered that such rumors would go around about them.

"Grandfather, I should have known you would want Dr. Emrys for our project. You could have saved me the trouble of getting settled in at the school had you told me they were to join us." Gabriella lovingly scolded Felix.

"I had no idea that the class you so wanted to take was Dr. Emrys, nor could I have told you that I had hoped to entice her to join our quest even if I had known." Felix replied.

"Well dear sister, don't I rate a hug as well?" Bruce questioned

As she released her grandfather to reply Adam instantly understood why Bruce had seemed so familiar to him. His warm dark eyes and smile were nearly as remarkable as Gabriella's. How could he have not put it together sooner? The two were exact complements: almost two parts of one whole now that he saw them standing together. Bruce had the same stunning eyes and easily likable inner love of life and strength as his sister. With all the excitement of being included on such a significant scientific expedition, Adam had nearly forgotten all about the lovely young Gabriella that he had been so taken with when he met her.

"Bruce, it has been so long." Gabriella said as she reached up to give him an equally warm embrace. "Younger or not, if you don't stop growing I am definitely going to have to start referring to you as big brother."

In some form of misplaced sense of protection towards Cordie, Heath's mood had immediately turned bitter at hearing Gabriella talk so casually about the rumors going around the university. He had not been particularly fond of Gabriella when they had met previously over his discovery of the tablets. She lacked her grandfather's tack and had immediately chastised him for removing them from the dig near the Bahariya Oasis without the proper people having been notified. If he had taken the prescribed steps of discovery they still probably wouldn't have even had a good chance at examining the tablets.

"I hate to break up this family moment," Heath said sharply, "but do you think we could get on with it. It's hot as hell out here and these bloody nats are driving me crazy."

Gabriella sent a cold dark look towards Heath. She still couldn't understand how her grandfather could stand to deal with such a despicable man. She knew both of the primary archeologists involved in the most recent digs at Bahariya. It angered her that she was forced to be deceptive by keeping quiet about the finds that Heath had removed without their knowledge. They were good men who had been looking for the tombs of El Bawiti's legendary governor, Zed-Khons-uef-ankh for years. It was appalling to Gabriella that someone like Heath would have stole such finds right out from under their noses.

"It is not enough that we have weeks of work in this dry environment, I thought we were not expecting your presents for some time yet Ms. Smith." Heath continued in an obviously distasteful tone.

Amehd took immediate offence at Heath's reaction to his home city. He turned away and began opening the doors to the large car in an effort to allow Gabriella and Dr. Emrys to embark. There was no love loss between most Egyptians and Dr. Heath Conrad. His destruction of valuable information while digging at varied Egyptian sites was well known and detested.

"You don't need to be rude Heath." Felix said simply and motioned to the others to move into the car. "You will show every member of this team and especially my granddaughter respect during this operation Dr. Conrad." Felix Smith added with great authority and unmovable determination. If anyone would be able to keep Heath Conrad in check, it would be Mr. Felix Smith.

Adam and Cordie were still speechless at the news that they were the topic of such outlandish rumors back at the university. How could they both have handled the situation so poorly? Neither said a word on the long drive from the airstrip to the Cairo Legacy House. Bruce had tried to add a little levity to the tension of the moment by leaning over to Adam and whispering, "A goddess huh!"

CHAPTER 11

It was a tense drive back through Cairo and to the large stone mansion of the Cairo Legacy House. The chaotic streets of Cairo were as always full of small automobiles honking their horns and swerving from crowded lane to crowded lane of traffic. In the midst of the modern city, farmers dressed in soft colored long cotton robes set atop wagons pulled by mules along the same crowded streets.

Cordie simply stared out the window in mortified silence as they drove through Cairo's Central Business District. Her mind was numbed by what she had overheard Gabriella saying. All she could do at the moment was watch the passing of the familiar old building along the road that she knew had been constructed in the late 1800s by Khedive Ismâ`îl on land reclaimed from swamps. Right now Cordie wouldn't have minded finding a swamp and just disappearing into it.

Adam felt equally bad but more so for Cordie than himself. He tried to concentrate on the sites along their drive. The first building on the left, he seemed to recall as the Cairo office of the Middle East Times. He remembered that it set between Shâri` Muhammad Sabrî Abû el `Alam and Shâri` Huda Sh`arâwî. The rest of the street they continued down slowly, curved along from Shâri` Huda Sh`arâwî to Shâri` el Tahrîr. For at least a few minutes Adam was able to concentrate on the remarkable crenellations on the buildings they passed. There was something peaceful about the way the curved streets drew his thoughts along. The only one of the group who had not spent enough time in Egypt to take in all the sights as commonplace was Denise. For her so much of this adventure would be new where as to the others it was less novel, at least at this point.

The Cairo Legacy House was an incredible stone mansion of alabaster colored rock and light wooden trims. Cordie had done a great deal of traveling prior to hiding away at the University and she even looked upon the Legacy House with awe. Unlike the castle in Scotland, there was a light warm appearance to the huge stone complex. And a complex it was indeed. The main entrance was near the center of a large traditional looking façade but there seemed to be at least three large wings reaching off in different directions.

"Oh grandfather if feels so good to be home again." Gabriella said in an almost girlish voice. "I stopped by as soon as my plane landed this morning and Jamila was already working in the kitchen. I could smell the spices of her cooking as soon as I opened the main door. Oh how I have missed Jamila and everyone here at home."

Bruce smiled warmly at his sister and there was finally a familiar smile back on Felix's face. It may be one of the grandest mansions Cordie had ever seen, but the Cairo Legacy House was definitely home for Felix and his grandchildren.

"Yes indeed Gabriella, a day hasn't gone by that Jamila hasn't reminded us that you would soon be back from the United States and she would have to have all your favorites baked and ready." Amehd added warmly. It was apparent that he was also very comfortable at the Legacy House, not to mention very well acquainted with the staff.

"Come help me with our equipment Adam." Bruce commanded as the rest of the group began getting out of the car and moving toward the main entrance. "Grandfather, I will show Adam to his room after we have everything out here stowed away. Which chamber did you intend for him?"

"The second down from your rooms would be fine son." Felix replied as he took Gabriella's arm and led the rest of the group up the winding stone pathway leading toward the main entrance.

"I thought we could use some time to talk over this reckless, not to mention rude Dr. Heath Conrad. What exactly do you know about him and he and Cordie's past Adam?" Bruce asked candidly as he opened the trunk of the car.

"To be perfectly honest Bruce, I don't know much about anything from Cordie's life prior to her coming to the university. I had never really realized how much I don't know about her until we began this trip." Adam said thoughtfully. He felt comfortable enough with Bruce to think out loud and not be too concerned with how Bruce took anything that he might say. "I can tell you, that beyond his notoriety within the scientific and academic world for being a very dislikeable person, Cordie had indicated a few times in the past that he was not someone she ever had the desire to run into again."

"I would imagine that most people who have spent any amount of time at all with him come to that very same conclusion." Bruce said causing both the young men to lighten up and laugh just a bit.

"Well, because grandfather had me help in preparing the background information on everyone he thought might be joining us on this project, I can tell you that there was a great deal more to their past together than Cordie has felt the need to share with you. I am only telling you this, because I did my best to not leave them alone together during our day in the caverns of Roslyn yesterday, but I am going to have my hands full playing buffer between him and all three of the others." Bruce began to explain.

"What do you mean, all three of the others? Whom are you talking about?" Adam questioned.

"The obvious is Gabriella, my dear sister has a great many talents and special gifts, but tack or patience with people that have caused her to mistrust them for any reason are neither to be counted among them.

She doesn't like Heath Conrad and I am afraid that is going to cause trouble. Secondly, and probably a little bit easier to handle is Amehd. You have to understand that Amehd is a very traditional Egyptian Muslims. He will take a lot, but he is proud of his home, his heritage and his faith and he detests everything that Heath Conrad is, greed, self serving, arrogance. The list could go on and on. It really came to a head between the two of them when Heath contacted the Legacy House to help him steal away the clay tablets. As much as Amehd wants to learn the knowledge and secrets of the mysteries of the tablets, he understands the importance they would serve to his government and the knowledge for future generations that such a find could hold if the whole site were not destroyed as Heath may have done."

Adam set down a heavy case that he had taken out of the trunk and turned to pay closer attention now to Bruce. "Even so, it is Cordie that you are the most concerned with, isn't it."

"Yes, I feel like I have to tell you what I know and ask for your help in keeping Heath away from her as much as possible under these conditions." Both men left the luggage and equipment they had been unloading set beside the car as they turned and walked a short distance further away from the main entrance.

Standing in the dry heat of the Egyptian sun, Adam looked intently at Bruce to go on.

"Did you know that Cordie was very high up in the Catholic Church? She was abandoned at birth and raised by Catholic nuns, then educated by the church. Evidently she even worked directly for the Vatican between her graduate and doctorial degrees. She had planned to take her vows as a nun on her 24th birthday."

"A nun? A Catholic nun?" Adam muttered almost to his self in disbelief.

"Well, I don't know of any other kind of nun in the Catholic church." Bruce replied sarcastically before continuing. "Again, from the best I can put together from the records grandfather had me searching, just months prior to her birthday and while exploring a find in Bolivar for the church, Cordie had the misfortune of running into Heath Conrad. He would have been only a couple of years older than her and I suppose might have even been considered charming to a young woman of Cordie's age. I don't know any of the personal details, but the long and short of it appears to be that Cordie fell in love, left the church all together and spent nearly three years with him in varied South American locations."

Bruce stopped at this point knowing that he had given Adam quite a shock. He looked at his new friend and waited to make sure he was prepared to hear more. When satisfied that he was, Bruce simply continued, "The break up was even more scandalous than the fact that she left the church and turned her back on her lifelong plan of taking the vows to become a nun. Again, evidently, from what I can make of the media coverage, Heath was after a very valuable relic and he intended to remove it from the people of the area and war basically broke out between Heath and Cordie about the sacred rights of the local population to the relic. I think it was a mask of some kind that the locals believed would allow the wearer to cross over to the realm of their dead ancestors and Heath believed was of gold and turquoise making it quite valuable. There was a very heavily covered media blitz where Cordie, probably rightfully so, accused Heath of being a thief and a danger to the local population. On the other side, Heath accused Cordie of being a naïve child of the church who was so emotionally troubled by not knowing who her parents had been that she was on a life long quest to answer the questions of our creation as a substitute. It seems to have gotten quite nasty, until Cordie just up and disappeared, giving up all efforts to help the local tribe. There was a period of about four years before she then showed up very quietly at the university."

Adam didn't even know where to begin with any kind of a response. He wasn't actually surprised that Heath Conrad could be such a devil, but he never in a million years would have suspect anything of the such from Cordie's background. He hadn't even known she had been raised an orphan. He actually began to feel a moment of foolishness that he had believed he and Cordie to be such close friends and coworkers when it was apparent he knew very little about the real woman under her professional persona.

Again, the two young men stood silently with the hot Egyptian sun beating down on them. Finally Bruce again took the lead and continued. "I can't imagine that it is easy for her to have to be working with him again. I think it is up to us to help make sure Heath Conrad doesn't put her into an uncomfortable position. Do you agree?"

"Yes of course. What is it you want me to do?"

"I don't know exactly." Bruce admitted. "I guess that if I am not around to keep things on a strictly business footing, you should try to step in and do the same. What I would really like, would be for you to help keep Gabriella from going after the man."

The mention of her name, Gabriella, immediately put a smile on Adam's tanned face. He looked up at Bruce and knew that he was probably even blushing a bit. "You had better never tell her what I had said about meeting her at the university," he warned.

That was enough to cause a small laugh between the two men. Bruce liked Adam and thought he was probably the best of any of the men his sister had dated, but this was not the time for romance. The job ahead of them was going to be difficult enough without a new budding romance beginning.

"Your secret about the dark eyed goddess is safe with me. Just remember that she is my sister." Bruce jested with Adam.

"Ah, I was hoping to run into you." Amehd's thickly accented voice sounded out from near the car. "I wanted to ask you about your name sir."

"Adam?" Adam replied puzzled.

Amehd smiled immediately showing a handsome full mouth of bright white teeth in contrast to his dark skin. "No of course not Adam. I was referring to your sir name, Khalid. Do you have an Arab or even more specifically an Egyptian heritage?"

The puzzled look on Adam's face broadened. He looked first at Bruce and then back to Amehd. "No, I don't believe so. Isn't that strange, me being a linguist and I have never even thought about my family name being anything but just our family name. "

"I am not sure of American names, but I am sure that Khalid is quite a common name among the Arab peoples." Amehd added.

"I am sure you are correct Amehd. Thank you for pointing that out to me. When all this is done, I may have to take some time to look into that. Maybe there is some Arab blood in my veins." Adam added sincerely.

"Now that you are out here Amehd, how about giving us a hand with this equipment?" Bruce said casually as the three moved back over toward the car.

CHAPTER 12

Cordie was getting settled into her lovely rooms. It was not just a single bedroom, but more of a small apartment of rooms for her own use. She had a small setting room with a dressing room off to the side and the main bedchamber on through a small corridor. She had her own bathroom and a small balcony. Everything was furnished in the finest soft mauve and light blue fabrics. There was a feeling of elegance that she did not believe she had ever felt.

It had been especially hospitable of Felix to suggest that she have a hot bath and take a nap prior to coming down for a late afternoon meal. The tensions of the morning had taken a lot out of her and there was something bothering her that she just couldn't put her finger on. Perhaps if she relaxed and pampered herself a bit her mind would be sharper and she would be able to figure out what it was.

Everything she could possibly need was provided for her. She sat down slowly at a beautiful pearl covered vanity table. She slowly picked up a golden handled brush and looked longingly into the mirror before her. Time seemed to stand still as Cordie brushed through her lustrous, golden blond hair in quiet meditation. Large blue eyes dominated her tired looking face, followed by subtle and somewhat common features. Her beauty had faded and was no longer obvious, not that she had ever been as alluring as either Gabriella or Denise. She wondered what Heath saw when he looked at her again; the tired looking middle aged woman looking back in the mirror at her now, or the youthful beauty she had once been.

After getting all of their luggage and equipment put away Bruce asked Amehd to show Adam to his rooms. "You know this old place as well as I do and if you don't mind I would like to have a talk with grandfather and Gabriella before we are all together again as a group later this afternoon."

"Not at all. I am happy to be of service." Amehd responded politely.

Bruce walked into his grandfather's study to find Gabriella already there. He walked in and tried his best to look at her through the eyes of someone other than her brother. No, he just couldn't see it. She was not an unattractive woman for a sister he supposed, but a goddess.

"What are you looking at? Do I have something on my face or something?" Gabriella asked at the strange was her brother was looking at her.

"Oh, no, I was just looking to see how you might have changes over the last few months sister dear." Bruce jokingly replied.

"How can you be in such a jovial mood Bruce? Haven't you had to spend the last day or so with that monster and his bimbo?" Gabriella challenged Bruce immediately.

"He isn't that bad if you just don't let him get under your skin Gabby. Why do you let him rub you the wrong way so easily? And what do you mean his bimbo?" Bruce knew that the best way to encourage his willful sister not to over react to Heath was to make it a challenge on her part. He wasn't at all sure he knew what she was talking about with the bimbo comment though.

"Give me a break Bruce, what else could the young journalist bring to this project. She is young, tall, and must make him feel like a real stud again."

"I can't believe the things that come out of your mouth!" Bruce admitted. "You would never know how educated and refined you are suppose to be to hear you talking. And who says he ever was 'a real stud'?"

"Have you seen the press on him 10 to 15 years ago. He has gotten into more diplomatic hot water over his attraction to women too young for him to be attracted to in at least a dozen different countries. Besides, I bet he wasn't too bad looking a few years ago." Gabriella laughed.

"You are just terrible sister of mine. What do you think grandfather would say if he heard you talking this way?" Bruce warmly scolded.

"He probably would tell me that I sounded like our mother. He has told me that many times over the last few years. He says that mamma was the only woman he had ever known that could talk papa under the table with her candor. I think he really misses both of them even more the older he gets." Gabriella said as her thought began to be calmed by her memories of her parents.

"I agree, he does miss them. Family is everything to grandfather and he is counting on us to carry it on." Bruce responded in an equally nostalgic tone of voice.

"Boy is that an understatement Bruce. That is what grandfather wants to talk to us about this afternoon. He will be down in a few minutes and I think he has decided to share with you even the most secret teachings that I have been schooled in. He has come to the conclusion that because we are twins and born just minutes apart that we should share in the family obligations that he has always referred upon me. I am going to tell you Bruce, it is a lot to take in all at once, but it will be great to have you to go through this together with."

Bruce didn't have any idea what exactly it was that Gabriella was making reference to but he believed it was more of what ever it was his grandfather had started to talk to him about last night in Scotland. Prior to Bruce being able to think of anything coy to say in response, the large doublewide oak doors opened and Felix walked into the study.

"What more could a man asked for, than to have both of his lovely grandchildren together with him again?" Felix asked rhetorically as he moved toward the small table and chairs that set in the west corner of the room. "Come set down with me. I have something of some significance to talk over with the two of you."

Bruce and Gabriella looked at each other and followed Felix to the table. The four chairs setting around the small square oak table were of great antiquity with Egyptian alabaster inlaid within the carvings along the side railings. The table was equally as handsome and made of the same fine light oak as the doors. There was one large book lying atop the table. It wasn't a volume that Bruce thought he had ever seen, but it did look at least to him that both Gabriella and Felix were familiar with it. Once all three had been seated, both his sister and grandfather almost systematically moved to lay their right hands on the cover of the book.

"Bruce, Gabriella has been schooled in the secret history of our heritage and family responsibilities. She has been given bits of knowledge and lessons in small amounts for many years. You unfortunately are not going to have the same benefit. I have decided that it is right that you should share this burden with your sister and in light of what we may be on the verge of discovering, you are going to have to take in all of the knowledge in one large, almost unbelievable helping. Do you think you can handle that son?" Felix asked as he paused and looked up at Bruce. Still, neither he nor Gabriella removed their right hands from resting on the book.

Even Bruce who could jest and joke his way out of almost any situation knew his grandfather all too well to make light of the moment. He set earnestly and simply shook his head almost unnoticeably.

"First you have to understand that everything I am about to tell you is fact. It is not merely legend, myth nor distorted historical misdirection. We are a very ancient family; more ancient than you could probably ever imagine. Even more imperative is that we are an ancient family with a very significant purpose here on this earth."

Bruce knew that the Legacy House had always been interested in historical mysteries and dug into lost mythological and archaic knowledge. He had seen for himself the results of many of the archeological expeditions that the Legacy House had funded. Still he had never been given any reason to believe that there was something more mysterious lurking behind the scenes of his family foundation. He continued to listen patiently to his grandfather.

Felix continued in a very soft, calm voice, "I know son that you have studied *The Secret Book According to John* as a part of your religious studies. I need you now to dig back in your memory son and try to recall all the details of the Gnostic revelations as presented in that text."

As he spoke, Felix lifted his left hand and softly laid it over Bruce's cupped hands resting in front of him on the oak table. The skin of the old man's hand was paper-thin with a smooth softness blanketing over Bruce's larger toughened hands. Within moments Bruce began to feel a physical energy flowing from his grandfather's hand into his own. It was a sudden yet very subtle and yet again very real presents flowing directly from Felix into Bruce.

"You must look deep into your memory to recall that in the Gnostic belief it was Wisdom or Sophia who caused, without the knowledge of God, Ialdabaoth to be created. Do you recall Bruce?" Felix said as he gripped Bruce's hands a bit tighter. "Ialdabaoth is real Bruce, very real."

Somehow Bruce knew that he was not expected to answer and just as mysteriously he began recalling in great detail the writings of *The Secret Book According to John*. God was the Parent of the Entirety or the First Principle, but he had not created our world as most schools of Christianity taught. God expanded into a full and complete nonphysical universe. It was the last of the aeons created by God, Wisdom, who gave birth to Ialdabaoth. Ialdabaoth was then the creator of the physical universe. He made the universe out of matter coping the perfect patterns of the spiritual universe. Ialdabaoth went on to create Adam, Eve, and their children along with the physical body and destiny as prisons for the human race. Abel and Cain were the result of a union between Eve and Ialdabaoth. It was only Seth, the third son of Eve that was a true result of a union between Adam and Eve.

Gabriella lifted her left hand and laid it over the mound of flesh under her grandfather's left hand. Bruce immediately felt the increase of the flow of energy he had begun feeling when his grandfather had first touched him. It was an overwhelming sensation running through every cell of his body, filling him with understanding and a peaceful acceptance.

"We are the offspring of the light, the seed of posterity and children of Seth. Our true home is the spiritual universe of light, not here in this material universe of darkness." Gabriella explained in a voice that echoed with a wise and noble tone.

Again in some unexplained manner, Bruce knew more than he should have been able to recall or remember. He could feel the sureness of what he knew deep within himself. It was almost as if a pocket of knowledge and understanding had been unlocked and allowed to seep out into his consciousness.

"I believe that we are on the verge with these new finds to reaching a point in time that God is calling for the world to awaken to the glory transmitted by the Gnostic race and penetrate the veil separating our universes." Felix concluded, "this may be the time that our race has existed for and you need to be ready to assist your sister."

The silence of the moments after Felix finish speaking seemed full of hope and mystery. Bruce knew without a doubt that he understood and had gained great knowledge seemingly through the touch of his sister and grandfather. What he still didn't know was, what the book their right hands rested on was nor how it fit into the transmission of this now so embedded knowledge he was experiencing.

CHAPTER 13

Cordie was resting comfortably in the warm scented water of her bath. The lovely soft scent of lavender rose from the warmth of the water surrounding her. She had pulled her hair up to keep it dry and allowed her small frame to sink deep within the warm comforting water. The last few days had been a whirlwind that she had never expected to be experiencing and it felt good to relax and get away from anything other than her own comfort and thoughts.

Then like an intruding stranger the idea of her ever being able to return to the university pushed its way back into her mind. She stretched her head back extending her neck and closing her eyes tried desperately to clear her mind again. It was no use. Somehow she had done it to herself all over again.

It had been hard enough to live down the scandal that surrounded her after leaving the church and then leaving Heath. She had done everything to make her life simple and unworthy of any real attention. The biggest controversy during the last ten years of her life had been the subject matter of her class and that she was perfectly comfortable with. She just couldn't understand how she could be finding herself back in this same undesirable position. What was it about her that caused her to find herself the subject of such gossip? Was this more punishment for her breaking her promise to God to become a nun and spend her life serving him?

Cordie realized that she had been laying in the tub long enough now that the water had lost it's lovely scent and nearly cooled. The skin on her fingers and toes were wrinkled and prune like. Still she had not come up with any answers to her damning questions. Concluding that she wasn't going to come up with any answers regardless of how long she stayed in the tub, Cordie decided to force herself up.

As she stood in the calf high water and watched droplets falling from her arms when she lifted them to move toward the towel something new began to crystallize in her mind. Finally a thought that wasn't disturbing to her. It was the keys, if they were crystals, as Heath believed, then they should have an energy of their own. The thoughts came rushing into her mind at a furious pace and the excitement began to reenergize her in a way the bath had not.

Bruce is a geologist she remembered. He would be the first to help her with the full implications of her thoughts. She couldn't wait until the afternoon meal to get on this. Maybe if she dressed and headed down to the main part of the house she would be able to find Bruce and try out her theory on him first.

Denise and Heath had used the time after arriving at the Cairo Legacy House to get settled into their rooms. Felix had given them more modest rooms in the research wing of the complex. There was a setting room between the two bedchambers that Denise and Heath could meet in. Heath knew that Felix had planned the accommodations this way in an effort to keep him as far away from Cordie as possible, but he didn't mind. In fact he counted it as a blessing that he and Denise would be out of earshot of the rest of the group.

"So Heath dear, it seems that you have more of an active interest in your old girlfriend than you had led me to believe." Denise playfully tugged at Heath's thoughts as she moved in closer to where he stood near his bed.

Heath moved only the upper portion of his fit and roughed body as he reached out and pulled Denise the remaining few inched toward him. His powerful arms encircled her young firm body as he pulled her chest in tight against his own.

"What kind of talk is that? I have one interest and one interest alone in the good Dr. Emrys. You on the other hand, keep my mind and body interested in a number of different ways." He responded just before kissing her passionately. Heath Conrad was far from a virtuous man but only in the presents of Denise did he speak so callously of Cordie. At one time they had seemed so close he remembered. Having been raised in privilege and in wealth, Heath had never understood the upbringing of a convent that had formed Cordie's believes. Her dedication to the service of others had been such a foreign concept to him even back then. Heath's first concern had always been for what he wanted in life, not what was right or would benefit other people. His roughed and mysteriously handsome looks had only aided his ease in pushing his way through life. Taller and stronger than most Heath also possessed a voice that was even deeper than most and to many always seemed to be bordering on arrogance.

After pushing any thought of Cordie out of his mind and within a few moments he reached his left arm down below Denise's bottom and swept her up into his arms, walked the couple of remaining steps and laid her on the bed.

He stood looking down at the lovely young woman full of desire for him. He should have been a very happy man, but although he would enjoy her, Heath knew that he would never see Denise as an equal in her own right. No, the only woman he had ever felt was his equal was Cordelia and that certainly wasn't in the cards for either of them.

Denise watched as Heath pulled of his shirt and then his jeans. She loved every bulging mussel, scare and mark on his body. She loved the way he touched her and added excitement to every aspect of her life. Only a few months ago she had been a recent graduate with a journalism degree and no real prospects for her future. Heath had taken her away from all that. Here she was in Cairo Egypt, having just left Scotland with the most exciting man she had ever known. Even more important to her was that he was a man who had included her in on his biggest discovery and if she did as he had told her before long she would be a world famous journalist in her own right.

Cordie had first gone back down to the main area of the house looking for Bruce. After not finding any sign of him, one of the servants had directed her to the research wing of the house. He had explained that Bruce had a laboratory in that portion of the house and she might be able to find him there.

As she was walking quietly down the wide corridor of the main floor of the research wing it was all coming together in her mind. The what that had been tugging on her earlier was now becoming more visible. There must be more to the key idea than just what Heath had mentioned. Crystals are the strongest concentration of energy ever found on the planet and if the keys were crystals then their power might be a treasure in its self.

All of the sudden Cordie realized that she had no idea where she was. She hadn't come upon any laboratory nor had she seen anyone along her route. What was it that the houseman had told her about finding the laboratory? Cordie stopped and looked at her surroundings. In the silence she heard something coming from on down the hall. She walked slowly toward the noise until she found herself close enough to make out the laughing voice of a woman.

"Heath, stop it! There isn't any more time. We need to get dressed and talk about this evening."

There was no doubt in Cordie's mind that it was Denise's voice. It was equally obvious that she and Heath were in bed together. Of all the things in the world, how could he be involved with someone that young and at such an important time? The whole idea infuriated Cordie. She couldn't remember the last time she had felt such immediate rage over something. No, that was not the truth, she knew exactly the last time she had felt this very kind of rage. It had been the last time she had allowed herself to be within 50 feet of Heath Conrad.

Suddenly her theory concerning the crystals could wait. She turned and quickly headed back down the corridor in the same direction she had come. Moving as quickly as she could without running Cordie put as much distance between herself and the sound of the girl's voice as possible.

CHAPTER 14

Felix was standing in the large open doorway of what must have been the dinning room talking to a small round faced older woman. The woman was modestly dressed in what appeared to Cordie to be a galabeyas. It was a lovely handmade dress of cotton and silk with delicate hand embroidered decorative stitch. Cordie caught her breath, straightened her blouse in an attempt to look settled and moved on toward Felix.

The olive brown skinned woman turned her attention to the approaching Cordie. The warmth of Jamila's smile seemed to transcend any of the other concerns within Cordie. She was nearly as old as Felix himself, but plump and full of life. Her eyes were dark and warm and the little bit of her hair not covered still shined of black mixed throughout the gray kept glossy from crushed rosemary oil.

"Cordie, dear, come let me introduce you to Jamila." Felix called out. "Jamila is in charge of the house and takes incredibly good care of the children and myself."

Jamila blushed a bit and lowered her eyes momentarily in the light of Felix's praise of her. She was a very proper Egyptian woman and as full of life as she was it would not have been proper for her to speak until Felix has finished.

"We are very honored to have you with us mam." Jamila said warmly.

There was just something so comforting and warm about Jamila that Cordie felt immediately at ease. "No, Jamila, it is I who am honored to be welcomed in your home. Thank you for your hospitality."

Felix smiled at the effect Jamila had on his guest. She had been a life saver when he had first moved Gabriella and Bruce into the Cairo house and by now he just considered her a part of his family.

"Jamila was informing me of the menu for the afternoon meal and breakfast in the morning. You are in for quite a treat Cordie." Felix said with pride, "Jamila's Egyptian kitchen is renowned for its tasty dishes. She has prepared some of Bruce's favorites not knowing that Gabriella would also be here. Today we will have Kofta and Kusheri. But she has ordered pigeon so that she can make Gabriella's favorite Hamam Mahshi, Stuffed Grape Leaves, Foul and Falafel tomorrow."

"Oh it has been so long since I last had stuffed pigeons. I will look forward to tomorrows meal as well Jamila." Cordie found herself saying directly to the lovely old lady. "Is there any possibility that you might be able to stir up some Mulukhia sometime during our stay?"

"Ah very possible indeed mam. The green soup is a simple dish and we always have the staples needed for Mulukhia. I am so please that you know and enjoy our Egyptian foods. Please let me know if you have any other requests."

The three were still standing talking together as the others began to come into the main area of the house. Gabriella was delighted to see Jamila. She nearly thought of the old woman as her mother and it had been too long since she had last seen her.

"Oh Jamila," Gabriella called out with delight. "I am so glad to be back home."

It was definitely the pride of a mother that Cordie now saw glowing in Jamila's dark eyes as Gabriella approached. She watched the two embrace and a hint of pain shot through her that she had never known her own mother.

"Dr. Emrys, I am so sorry to have spoken so poorly earlier this morning." Gabriella said sincerely as she straightened up from her hug with Jamila. "I truly couldn't have spoken with less concern for your feelings and I am terribly sorry."

"Oh Gabriella, thank you but your apology is completely unnecessary and it is Cordie." Cordie returned just as sincerely. Then with hesitation she added not really knowing why, "Was it really as bad as you made it sound this morning?"

Gabriella laughed at Cordie's ability to ask such a question. She was taking an immediate liking to this older woman.

"I can't imagine why you would not want everyone back at that stuffy university to think that you might have run off with me." Adam added to the jest as he came up behind the small group.

Gabriella turned and smiled warmly at Adam. "Nor can I Dr. Khalid." She announced playfully and seductively. There was already something very familiar and relaxed about the way that she felt towards Adam. She almost felt as at ease with him as she did her own twin brother.

Adam blushed at her attention but tried once again to act professional and competent. Neither of which he was able to pull off. "So this is the family that you had a family obligation to, that need to take you away from our class for two weeks?"

"You two have met?" Cordie asked quickly.

The two looked at each other, smiled knowingly and at almost the same time replied, "yes" giving no other explanation.

Adam was pleased to see Gabriella take a seat for lunch next to his. She truly was as lovely and enchanting as he had first imagined and to be a part of this project and Felix's granddaughter she must also have a brain worth exploring. As soon as everyone had been seated Jamila rang a soft bell and three male servants dressed in white cotton began to serve the meal.

Bruce smiled and gave Jamila a wink as his favorite ground meatballs were set down before him. It was very nice to see his sister paying attention to a man as likable as Adam and having such a fine meal put before them all. After everything that he had learned about himself and his family only a few hours ago, Bruce was looking at almost everything from a different perspective. Could grandfather be right? Was their existence in this material universe going to change and were they going to find their way to true enlightenment and an existence with God in the spiritual universe? It was just all too much to contemplate and understand right at the moment and besides, he simply couldn't wait to dig into the Kolfa on his plate.

"Now that Gabriella is with us earlier than originally thought possible, how should our timetable be adjusted, if at all?" Felix began the work session by asking.

"The key is in finding the crystals. When are we scheduled to make the attempt to retrieve them?" Heath asked next.

"According to my calculations it isn't precisely beneath the Sphinx that we will find ourselves." Amehd began.

Heath immediately jumped in, in a harsh accusative tone, "Of course it is beneath the Sphinx. What are you talking about?"

Felix sent a sharp look down the table at Heath, which was all it took to quiet him. "Please go on Amehd." Felix said.

"As most of you would already know, in the Kore Kosmou we are told 'As above, so below' and the Roman historian Ammianus Marcellinus wrote of great subterranean passages and winding retreats built by men before the flood to house documents, 'lest the memory of all their sacred ceremonies should be lost'. Some of you may even know that one of the sacred names of the Sphinx is neb. Neb means the spiraling force of the universe," Amehd explained.

Heath could not help himself. His inpatients and need to be right out weighted the warning that Felix had given him with his sharp look. He interrupted saying, "Just more reason to believe that the passages lie under the Sphinx."

"As I said prior, not precisely Dr. Conrad." Amehd continued in a manner that revealed none of his great distaste for Heath. "Do you know what a Fibonacci spiral is?

Not waiting for a response Amehd continued, "It is kind of a phi-controlled spiral. If we draw a Fibonacci spiral that would touch the apex of all three Giza pyramids, it folds in on itself at a more precise location south-east of the pyramids, between the Sphinx and the Nile."

"Didn't I read something about red granite being found some years back by the Egyptian Ministry of Irrigation? I seem to recall that is was a type of red granite that would have been brought up from Aswan in the south." Bruce added, "the location was in front of the Sphinx and it was suggested that it could be the roof of some type of underground building."

"Yes that is correct Bruce," Amehd continued. "There has also been ground penetrating radar used to locate what is believed to be a horizontal passageway that connects the end of the descending passage of the Great Pyramid to the known underground chamber. A structure that very well could be a corridor crossing the horizontal passageway at an angle of about 45 degrees seemed to lead directly to the Sphinx."

Again, Heath's inpatients overtook him, "We all agree that the Giza plateau is honeycombed with underground tunnels. That is why we practiced in the duplicate tunnels constructed as a map under Roslyn. None of this makes any difference. The only real question is whether or not we are going to be able to get into the tunnel behind the northwest rear paw? Who gives a damn where we are underground after that point, as long as it leads us to the crystal chamber."

"Amehd has made all the arrangements just as we had asked of him. If you feel we are ready we can be under the Sphinx tonight." Felix replied sharply again displeased with Heath's behavior.

"We're as ready as we can possibly be. We know the labyrinth as we expect it to be and if our theory is right we should be able to find the inner chamber just as we practiced in Scotland. And if we are wrong we are going to need as much time as possible to try to come up with an alternative location." Heath added quickly.

"Alright let us recap." Felix moved on to clarify the situation. "We have a very strong belief in the translation of at least five of the seven groupings on the clay tablet. The clay tablet with the map of the Nile valley indicates that the crystals should be located below ground somewhere in the vicinity of the Sphinx. If we do find the crystals there is no reason that we can not continue our work from the jet and move on to South American now that we do not have to wait for Gabriella."

"Felix, I haven't had the opportunity to run this theory by Bruce yet, but I think that when we find the crystals we are going to find more than simple pieces of stone." Cordie interjected, "Crystals are known to store and carry great energies. If these crystals are pure we may find them alive with a very powerful form of energy."

It was not Bruce, but Adam that spoke up first. "Cordie that is incredible, I was just reading in one of the ancient language banks early this morning about the belief that crystals were used as storage devices in ancient times."

Gabriella waited for Adam to finish and then added, "there are many ancient myths and believes that talk of the power of crystals found naturally within the earth."

"I think this is very significant, but will it have any effect on how we handle the crystals when we find them?" Heath asked directly.

Everyone thought for a few minutes about his question and then it was Bruce who spoke up. "From a geological perspective any energy found in the crystals themselves would not be harmful to human touch. At the most the crystal might vibrate or hum slightly, but unless there is some high degree of heat emanating from the crystals than there should be no danger that I can think of."

"Alright then Amehd can you contact the guards that it will be tonight." Felix concluded. "Adam, Gabriella can show you to the primary computer room and help you with your continued effort to translate the table. The rest of us can have the evening at leisure and we will all meet back at the main entrance at 11 pm."

Adam was delighted to have any excuse to talk alone with Gabriella. He couldn't believe the effect she had on him. There was just something so refreshing and enticing about her. He wasn't sure what he wanted to say to her; it was just that he knew he wanted to be near her. Gabriella didn't seem to mind being alone with him either.

"This is quite and impressive lab." Adam commented as they walked into the large open room. The computer terminals were positioned around the outer walls with a large projection screen on the north wall. It was clear that the most advanced technology available any where in the world was represented here at the Cairo Legacy House.

Gabriella replied modestly, "Grandfather has always tried to make sure we have what ever might be helpful in our efforts."

Adam could hardly keep his mind on the conversation for wanting to comment on the sparkle emanating from the dark pools of her eyes. He made his best attempt by asking, "and what are your efforts? I mean, what is it that the Legacy House represents?"

Gabriella knew she could not disclose everything, but surely her grandfather trusted this young man or he wouldn't be a part of this expedition. She thought for a few minutes then playfully replied, "our relationship with God of course."

Seeing that Adam didn't look too alarmed she went on. "I mean simply that the Legacy House's roots lie in the remote past and it has always carried a strong sense of a particular knowledge and possession of some secret traditions. It is just that we don't know exactly what all of that knowledge or secret tradition is other than that it centers around human kinds relationship with God."

"That makes the Legacy House seem more like a religious foundation than the scientific foundation I have always believed it to be." Adam replied.

"Is there really a big difference?" Gabriella curiously replied. "I mean can you have religion without science or science without religion?"

"I think a large portion of the population of the world would say that indeed you can and that one contradicts the other." Adam added.

"So they might, but those are the unacquainted as grandfather would say." Gabriella paused and looked intently into Adam's eyes. "But I don't believe that you nor Dr. Emrys think that way at all. I believe that you are much more aware of your acquaintance than either of you may realize."

Adam wasn't completely sure what Gabriella meant, but he certainly liked the way she was looking at him. He felt like she could see deep inside and that there would be no use at all in trying to hide anything from this remarkable woman.

CHAPTER 15

Cordie, Gabriella and Denise were all wearing identical black jeans and black t-shirts, which only seemed to emphasize to Cordie just how much smaller she was then either of the younger women. Both Gabriella and Denise seemed to have legs nearly as long as Cordie was tall, or at least it seemed that way to her as they moved away from the car. They had parked nearly a half-mile from the Pyramid site and would have to walk the remaining distance. It was close to 1 a.m. but Amehd had explained that they could not risk beginning any earlier do to the late night laser light show presented for the tourist at the Pyramid. The guards that Amehd had bribed to look the other way told him that they would take a coffee break precisely at 1:45 a.m. so they didn't have a lot of time to waste.

Heath had been instructed by Felix not to say a word. Even with the arrangements that Amehd had made with the guards, if they had known that Heath Conrad was one of the group they were allowing to sneak into the Pyramid complex the whole deal would have been off. Bruce and Gabriella led the way around the side of the steep embankment they had come upon. The village of Nazlet-el-Samaan rested quietly below the embankment that led to the Pyramid's north face.

The silence of the still night was interrupted quickly by the sound of men. Three armed guards were muttering amongst themselves about 50 yards ahead. The men wrapped in blankets against the chill of the night air were sharing a cigarette and conversing quietly. Bruce raised his hand to indicate to everyone behind him to stop. Everyone, even Heath stood motionless for the time being in the shadow almost afraid to even breath. Bruce could see the overwhelmingly huge bulk of the Pyramid reaching up into the night sky as they hid just out of range from the security lights. It seemed as if time stood still until finally one of the guards picked up his shotgun, looked at his watch and indicated to the other two men that it was time to go.

Bruce waited until the guards were entirely out of site to begin moving forward. All eight figures dressed in black silently made there way through the soft sand around the northeastern corner to the eastern face of the Great Pyramid.

It was incredible; everything was exactly as Heath had explained it. Climbing into the main chamber of the pyramid they quickly made their way through two stone plugs that more than likely had not been moved for thousands of years. Once past the last secret plug the tunnels made the exact same twists and turns as those beneath Roslyn. How could such intricate details all be so exact? They could have been blindfolded and made their way effortlessly through the maze of tunnels and pathways running further and further down into the depths of the earth. There was no way of telling from underground whether Heath or Amehd had been correct in the exact positioning of the tunnels. They had made so many twists and turns that no one could assuredly know whether they would end up under the Sphinx or at some point out further in the desert as Amehd had predicted.

Bruce stopped and motioned for Heath to move up and take the lead. As detestable as Heath had been, this was his area of expertise. He had been the one mapping out the labyrinth beneath the Scottish chapel at Roslyn and it was only right that he should be to one to lead the group through the passages to the underground chambers of the Sphinx. Bruce also wanted to keep a closer eye on his grandfather during the climb.

Heath smiled that devilishly sly smile of his as he passed Cordie to take his place in the lead. She couldn't help but be attracted by that smile, almost as if time hadn't passed and she was still the young naive girl she had been when she had first seen it. It aggravated her that he still had any effect what so ever on her, but there was still a small part deep within her that enjoyed seeing Heath in the lead where he was most accustom to being.

The group moved down into the main tunnel where the ground leveled out and finally felt safe turning on their lights. As the perfect stone walls of their surroundings became visible in the yellow light of their lamps Cordie let out a slight sigh of disbelief. Again, Heath had been correct, the detailed paintings on the tunnel walls matched exactly the photos of Roslyn they had studded.

"I think we are well out of any hearing range down here. We should be able to talk freely without fear of being discovered. My best guess is that no one has been down in these tunnels for thousands of years." Felix said.

It was Denise who spoke next. The sound of her voice still irritated Cordie but at least this time, she was being of some help. "If we are to get what we have come for and be out before dawn we had better get to it. I'll get the pictures we need in here and you should all follow Heath toward the crystal chamber."

"If there is a crystal chamber." Adam mumbled to himself. He still hadn't gotten over his suspicions towards Heath nor had he forgotten how the overly confident egotistical monster had lashed out at Gabriella. He was finding himself more and more protective of Gabriella.

Bruce had heard Adam's comment and patted him in a friendly fashion as he encouraged his young friend to continue moving forward. "Let's hope for our sakes he is correct this time my friend." Bruce whispered back.

It took nearly another 30 minutes of steady movement before Heath found himself standing before a large stone door. It truly was here, right where it should have been. He held his breath as he began pushing open the perfectly placed solid stone door.

At first his efforts yielded no response. The door was enormous, at least twice the size of the stone block placed as the door of the inner chamber under Rosslyn Chapel. There were no signs what so ever of the stone having ever been moved. It was set solidly into the cut and polished stone of the chamber walls. Both Adam and Bruce moved forward to assist Heath in his efforts to open the stone door.

As the door slowly gave to the men's pressure a gleaming stream of light rushed through the opening. Heath knew that the maps had been correct and he was about to be the first man in literally thousands of years to see the glory of what the ancients had left behind. For the first time in his life, Heath Conrad felt unsteady and cautious about his next move. Adam and Bruce both stepped back as Heath turned and called back to Felix, "We're here, the door is right in front of me. You had better get Denise up here so we can get pictures as we enter."

Felix did just as Heath had suggested and he and Denise moved past everyone else to the front of the tunnel. "I can't believe you waited Heath, maybe I am getting through to you after all." Felix jested.

Denise poised herself ready to get the pictures. This was the moment that Heath had brought her along for. She would never take more important pictures than the ones she was about to snap.

Felix stood just behind Heath as he pushed the door further open. The light exploding within the chamber was nearly blinding. Both men reached up and turned off the lights on their helmets as they forced their way into the bright barrier the crystals were giving off. Once the yellow rays of their lights were gone, the pure white light from the crystals seemed to soften themselves. The uncontaminated light of the crystals themselves seemed to begin to dance warmly in hues of pink and lavender around the small chamber they were housed in. There were three separate crystals, each standing on a pure gold pedestal in the center of the chamber.

Denise moved in to take pictures before even Heath moved to touch the crystals. As Felix had reassured him, once enough photographic evidence had been obtained, Heath was the first to be allowed to reach out and lightly touch the center crystal. There was no heat radiating from the crystal. It was smooth and perfectly cool to the touch. Heath lifted the central crystal from its pedestal and held it close to his left ear.

"Cordie was right, there is a steady vibration. It isn't really a sound, but I know that it's there just as she had predicted." Heath said with a mixture of delight and amazement in his voice. "Cordie come up here. You have to experience this yourself."

Cordie moved quickly in next to Heath. The chamber was hardly large enough for four of them to stand in at any one time and she found herself being pushed up close to Heath's chest as she reached out to take the crystal from him. He smiled at her as if she was the only person in the world as he placed the precious crystal in her tiny hand and followed it with his own up to her right ear.

"Yes, yes that is just what I expected. Do you know what this means Heath? Do you all understand the significance of what we have found?" Cordie said with immense joy in her soft voice.

Gabriella and Adam were the last to make their way into the chamber to see the resting place of the two remaining crystals. Felix, Heath and Cordie had all moved out into the open chamber to allow each of the group to examine the find and have Denise photograph their experience. Adam first noticed the soft colors of the crystals as they sent sparkles into Gabriella's dark eyes. He was of course moved by the experience of seeing the crystals resting as they had for ages on their golden pillars, but it was the breathtaking beauty and innocence of Gabriella's eyes that still captured the moment in his heart. He wished with all his heart that he had the nerve to tell her how he felt.

"Come on you three, we have to secure the crystals and head back if we are to get out and back to the car before dawn." Felix called out softly to them. Then as an afterthought, Felix added, "Amehd I think it would be a good idea to take one of the gold stands for tests. We will make sure that afterwards it gets returned or turned over to the proper Egyptian authorities."

Adam took both of the crystals from their perch and handed one to Bruce just as had been planned. Gabriella helped Adam wrap his remaining crystal in the soft cloth Ahmed had brought with them and then slid it neatly into his backpack. Cordie had done the same to help Bruce with his crystal and they were finally all ready to head back through the labyrinth toward the exit they had marked near the base of the Sphinx.

The drills that Heath had put them all through no longer seemed so ridiculous. In fact Heath didn't even seem quite so terrible to most of them as they triumphantly made their way with ease back through every twist and turn needed to take them directly to their point of exit.

CHAPTER 16

The next few days seemed to pass without notice. Everyone was working on their own pieces of the puzzle. It was Amehd who was handling the evaluation of the golden stand they had retrieved from the inner chamber beneath the Sphinx. Just as Felix had suspected the gold proved to be unnaturally pure. Amehd had heard of some very rare pieces of Egyptian jewelry made of virtually pure gold. The significance as Bruce had verified was that it is impossible to make gold by any normal metallurgical process due to the need to remove various impurities in the ore. The only known method would have involved heating gold until it vaporized, like liquor in a still. Then the vapors would have to be allowed to cool, leaving behind the impurities. It was unthinkable that any ancient civilization would have had the knowledge to produce the immensely high temperature required for such a process. But how else could this pure form of gold be explained?

Amehd had a great deal of respect for his ancestors and pride in all that they knew. Still he could not bring himself to believe that they had worked with temperatures that would have needed to be the equivalent of 6,000 degrees Celsius. This would almost be like his ancestors possessing something along the same lines as atomic power.

Denise had found an article in a reputable science magazine that made reference to a similar mystery. It spoke of a necklace made of pure gold that had been found in Mexico. She had also been able to dig up for him a record from the British Museum. It verified that the museum had sent some iron tools from Egypt to a metallurgist some years back. To the astonishment of the experts it seemed to prove that the ancient Egyptians were using powdered metallurgy, a process that involves heating the metal to a temperature where it vaporizes, then condenses in the form of a powder. A scientist in the records stated that the Egyptians had obtained the required temperatures, by the same processes that made the atomic bomb possible; atomic fission.

Amehd was still not sure what to make of all these scientific anomalies, but he firmly believed that it was all a piece of Felix's puzzle centered around forgotten, or suppressed human knowledge. He also knew that Felix had secrets that he kept from even him. Where was all of this going to lead them?

Bruce had continued his research on the possible evidence of some very well organized and advanced mapping of the earth by ancient civilizations and with Amedh he could now try to put a theory together that would include the mathematical and astronomical implications.

They had found the crystals but they still didn't know exactly where the next site was located. In other words, they had the keys but didn't know what they unlocked. There were references on the tablet to the Seven Caves, but no one really knows where the fabled Seven Caves are located.

Amehd had been working on the mathematics of the idea that the ancients had left a worldwide grid of secret sites, kind of as geological makers. He was finding excellent evidence of a mysterious web of sacred sites scattered around the globe in very precise locations linked by sacred latitudes.

"Amehd, are you sure that all of these locations are 10 phi locations?" Bruce asked in amazement as he reviewed Amehd's findings with him.

"Oh yes very sure Bruce." Amehd replied with confidence. "Today Lubaantum, Tiahuanaco and Raiatea are all at 16:11N or 10 Phi latitude. During the Hudson Bay Pole it would have been Baalbek, Paracas and Cuzco and even more telling, during the Yukon Pole it would have been Yonaguni and Lixus."

"This is truly unbelievable information Amehd." Bruce commented distantly as he continued to examine Amehd's findings. "Here explain these location here. What is this Equatorial Golden Section you have indicated?"

Amehd had great respect for Bruce and didn't mind explaining his finding to him at all. He went on to explain his list of lost sacred sited linked simultaneously to the Giza prime meridian along with the current and the former position of the earth's crust/mantle as it had shifted. That was something that Bruce had a firm understanding of, the theories on the crust displacement of the earth causing locations around the globe to have shifted into other locations. "Here at the 30W location of the Giza Prime Meridian the Sahara Desert and Canterbury would coincide with these other 10 phi sites of the Hudson Bay Pole sites; Baalbek, Cuzco, Ollantaytambo, Paracas, Sidon, Nineveh, Machu Picchu and Ehdin, all ancient sacred sites.

"Since grandfather is sure we are looking for a site in either Central or South America, maybe we should focus on the sites in Peru such as Cuzco, Ollantaytambo, Parcas and Machu Picchu rather than Baalbek which is in Lebanon along with Sidon. I think for our immediate purposes we can also rule out Nineveh. There is little possibility that we are looking for an Assyrian city and I don't think we want to look toward Iraq at this point. Would you agree?" Bruce said as he looked up for Amehd's reaction.

"I would indeed. Shall we present Cuzco, Ollantaytambo, Parcas and Machu Picchu to the group at today's review meeting?" Amehd replied with agreement.

Just as Amehd had finished talking Denise suddenly appeared at the door. She was carrying a folder of information that she had finally been able to pull together on the subject of Uriel's Machine. She looked uneasy and suggested that she just leave the information and they could discus it later.

Bruce and Amehd were so involved in the current issues at hand that neither even tried to convince her to stay and explain her findings. Instead Bruce simply took the folder and tucked it under his arm as they waited and watched Denise turn and leave them.

"Let's find Cordie and take a look at the six original maps Heath dug up with clay tablets." Bruce added as if Denise had never interrupted them..

Cordie had been anxious to see the maps and welcomed Bruce's suggestion. Amehd and Cordie waited behind Bruce as he punched a security code into a panel near one of the doors off his laboratory. To both their astonishment the loud sucking sound of an air lock chamber preceded the opening of the door.

Once inside Bruce led them to six airtight glass trays that appeared to be suspended in mid air. "As soon as Heath uncovered the maps and they were exposed to the air they began dissolving at an alarming rate. That was when he called Grandfather for help. He knew that he did not have the means to protect the maps from destruction. A part of me still thinks that Grandfather should have just taken the maps into protection and then turned Heath Conrad over to the authorities. I wasn't here at the time, but I understand the Gabriella really let Heath have it with a verbal whipping when she saw the decay of this first map. It took the worst of it because it was on the outside of the roll when Heath pulled the maps from inside some kind of barrel or tube."

Cordie couldn't believe what she was hearing. It was yet another example of just how irresponsible Heath was. Any credible archeologist would have known how to secure the site before removing anything just to avoid this type of situation. Still, even with the damage done to the first map, it was clear to her that these were the most detailed maps of the world that she had ever seen. They were more precise in their focus on locations and their perspective relationship to different planet and star grouping alignments than most of the similar work done today. Each map showed what appeared to be a progressive evolution of what the earth would have looked like during six varied periods of major earth changes.

Amehd was equally astonished by the complexity of the maps. It was more than obvious that some ancient people had known much more about the size and make up of the earth and the shifts and displacement of the crustal movement than the scientists of today. Still after very careful examination by all three it was agreed that the maps did not give them any better indication of where they would find the Seven Caves.

The folder of information that Bruce had continued to hold under his arm slipped loose and fell to the floor. Several article clippings and printouts scattered about as they hit the floor. Cordie immediately recognized the article titles and bent down to get a closer look.

"Uriel's Machine," Cordie said thoughtfully. "Where did all of this information come from?"

"Denise brought it to us just as we were about to leave to come find you. We haven't even had a chance to look it over yet. Does it look as if there is anything useful?" Bruce added as he and Amehd joined Cordie on the floor.

"I think so, look at this." Cordie said and then began to read from one of the clippings, "Lomas and Knight have constructed 'Uriel's machine' for studying the heavens, and they also deduced, from the words of the prophet Enoch, at what latitude the machines must have been locate…"

Amehd was already lost in the research findings. He was reading with great enthusiasm the copy of an article on Uriel's machine Damian Thompson that quoted archaeologist Tim Schadler-Hall saying that in East Yorkshire there is an unbroken geological record of centuries before and after 7,460 BC. Amehd had met Tim Schadler-Hall and knew of his work as being very complete. He was acknowledging that through the study of the simple arrangement of posts or standing stones for studying the heavens that has been named Uriel's machine, that the ancients had the ability to monitor changes within the earth such as the earth's mantle beginning to move.

"With Uriel's machine it appears that there is little doubt that the idea of sacred sites around the world have been specifically placed at designated latitude points." Amehd finally said. "Do you realize Bruce that Uriel's machine seems to have been designed to used the position of the stars to monitor the movements of the inner earth. It was probably the first ancient seismic device that could be used to anticipate crust displacement. This completely blends astronomy and math with the science of geology and proves the importance of phi, 5- and 10-degree intervals."

Bruce and Cordie both had to agree with the significance that Amehd had found in the research. Cordie could not help but think of it in terms of even more proof and validity toward the Book of Enoch being a description of God sending his angles down to earth to show and instruct humankind. She knew that Uriel was one of the Watcher angles that had been sent to earth to keep an eye on the rebellious angles and guide Enoch.

"Well, I guess our photojournalist has come through with more than we expected from her. I think this information strengthens even more the discussions Amehd and I were having earlier." Bruce concluded.

"So we are back to the original suggestion." Amehd finally said. "Do we agree then that we should bring up the Peruvian locations for discussion at today's meeting?"

"I think so, at least it is a start and we can get everyone thinking about what those sites might have in store for us. Good work Amehd. We are lucky to have you working with our group." Bruce said in a sincere manner.

"No sir, it is I who am fortunate to be included. Your grandfather has been quite good to me and I only wish to be of assistance in his efforts." Amehd replied in an equally sincere manner.

Cordie had not seemed to hear a word that either man had said. She was still too absorbed in her own thought of Enoch and the reality of his books.

CHAPTER 17

Cordie had been staying as clear of Heath and Denise as possible. It wasn't hard to keep herself buried in the work at hand during the day and she simply worked herself until she was so tired that she fell fast asleep at night. It was only during the daily review meetings following the large afternoon meal that she really had to spend any significant time in their presents.

Today Jamila had as she had promised prepared the delicious green soup that Cordie had requested. That, along with the fact that she had finally seen the source maps was enough encouragement to satisfy Cordie and put her in more agreeable mood for the afternoon meeting. She had not had Mulukhia this good in she really didn't know how long.

"Thank you Jamila, the Mulukhia is wonderful." Cordie said as she finished her second bowl.

Jamila smiled and lowered her eyes in humble acceptance of the complement.

"Are we ready to review where we each are at this point?" Felix asked as he did everyday at about this time. That was his subtle way of informing everyone that the meal was ending and the meeting was about to begin.

The savants poured thick black coffee into the small crystal cut glasses and cleared the plates so that the meeting could begin. The excitement of finding the crystals had somewhat subsided and now everyone seemed impatient to discover just where they were to jet off to next.

"Grandfather, Amehd has done incredible work and we have four sites in Peru that we think the group should discus." Bruce began.

"Peru, no that isn't right!" Heath shouted in irritation.

Everyone in the room held their breath to see what example of bad behavior Heath was going to demonstrate next. Denise even seemed taken back by his out burst.

"I have covered Peru from top to bottom and the Seven Caves are not in Peru." He said in only a slightly calmer voice.

"No one said the Seven Caves are going to be found in Peru. What I did say and expect to have considered prior to rash judgments is that we have four sites in Peru that we would like to have the group discus." Bruce said firmly but without the same kind of uncontrolled rage that Heath had demonstrated.

For the first time since Cordie and Adam had met Felix they saw him actually get angry. "I have had enough of this," he said as he put his fist down on the table. "Bruce go on and Dr. Conrad if you can not respect the opinions of the rest of the group you may excuse yourself immediately."

"What are the Peruvian sites Bruce?" Gabriella asked in an attempt to take attention away from Felix and get the discussion moving forward. She could see that her grandfather was not looking at all as composed or in control as he normally did. His aged hands were still shaking from his anger and that just simply was not at all in character for him.

"Cuzco, Ollantaytambo, Parcas and Machu Picchu" Bruce added dryly.

That was all it took. Heath stood up and without another word marched out of the dining room. There was a minute or two of deathly silence before Gabriella spoke next.

"Before we begin again and are interrupted again, don't you want to run after your companion Denise?"

Denise looked totally shocked by Gabriella's comment, as did nearly everyone else in the room for that matter. She gave a very innocent tilt of her lovely head and replied, "I don't know what you intended to mean by companion, but Heath and I are professional colleges only. I would like to stay and participate in the meeting if that is alright with everyone else."

Cordie now had undeniable proof that the very innocent acting Denise was lying through her perfect white teeth. Everyone else in the room might have felt at least a bit sorry for the way Gabriella had attacked Denise, but Cordie knew it was not nearly all the girl deserved. She didn't trust her and she especially didn't trust her and Heath Conrad together.

Before anything else could be said Cordie jumped in on behalf of Gabriella saying, "Well then if we aren't to have any further interruptions I'll begin with a question. What is it about these four locations that have drawn them to your attention?"

"Very good question." Amehd replied. He went on to explain, "A Golden Section is something that is consistent any-where in the universe no matter what the number system being used, base 10, 12, 60 or etc. If an ancient yet very advanced civilization was trying to make contact with people in the future they would have realized that those people might not use the same weights and measures that they themselves had used. Two things that would never change would be the dimensions of the earth and the geometry of the Golden Section. In other words the distance from the equator to the pole will never change no matter what number system you use and that distance will always be able to be divided by the Golden Section. Cuzco in the Andes is such a site. Using mathmatics, the only constant language we have determined that Cuzco, Ollantaytambo, Parcas and Machu Picchu were all phi 10 locations. It is in following the same mathematical evidence that led us to the crystal chamber."

"Well, I can relay the legend of how Cuzco evolved into one of the most sacred cities in the Andes." Codie then offered.

"That would be a good start Cordie. Please do." Gabriella encouraged.

"The basic tradition is that after the great flood The Sun sent two of his children, Manco Capac and Mama Oello Huaco to gather the natives into communities and teach them the arts of civilized life. They advanced along the high plains in the area of Lake Titicaca to about the sixteenth degree south. They were said to have bore with them a golden wedge, and had been instructed to take up residence on the spot where the sacred emblem should without effort sink into the ground. When they reached the valley of Cuzco the miracle of the wedge speedily sinking into the earth and disappearing happened. So at Cuzco the children of the Sun established their home."

"I seem to recall that the golden wedge was also sometimes referred to as the golden wand and was thought to be some kind of homing device that led the Children of the Sun directly to Cuzco." Gabriella added.

"That is correct my lady, and Cuzco is related to both the Hudson Bay and Yukon poles." Amehd went on to include in the discussion, which was now flowing freely as all had hoped for.

"The Inca Trail which was one of the great wonders of the ancient world ran from Cuzco in the south to Quito in the north." Bruce said.

Cordie went on to take Bruce's thought a step further by adding, "That is right Bruce. And it is beginning to appear that information buried at Cuzco before the flood may have provided the ancient people with a plan for laying out the post-flood sacred sites. Amehd had shown us that a link can be made of Cuzco to Tiahuanaco and Cuzco to Quito causing the 45 degree lay line connecting these ancient sacred sites to make perfectly good geodetic sense. As far as that goes, Ollantaytambo and Machu Picchu are so close to Cuzco that they should be considered a grouping. Remember it is at Ollantaytambo that the largest stones ever used in construction of any site in the New World were quarried on the mountainside on the opposite side of the valley."

"Red granite blocks of enormous size were hewed and shaped then transported from the mountainside, across two streams before carefully being raised and put precisely in place in the building of Ollantaytambu." Bruce again added.

Felix stood and straightened his tailor vest. Gabriella could see that his hands were still trembling slightly but he seemed to be much more himself as he said, "I believe that you are all on the right track with this, however, I must agree to some small degree with Heath that we do not know how this all fits into our search for the Seven Caves or our mission there with the crystals. I am afraid that until we have more information on the meaning of the last two groupings of the clay tablet we are only going to be going in circles. Adam, son, how are you coming with that effort?"

"Not as well as I would have hope." Adam had to admit. There seemed to be something completely different within the last two groupings. He had not yet figured out how to make the transfer from the first five to the sixth and seventh.

"That is alright son." Felix said very reassuringly. "You'll get it, just keep working on it and if there is anything that you need from any of the rest of us, please don't hesitate to ask."

With that Felix turned and walked very slowly and in a deliberate manner out of the dinning room. He was tired and felt that he needed to rest a bit.

CHAPTER 18

Denise remained with the group for far longer than she would have normally. She hadn't liked Gabriella's implication and wanted to do everything that she could not to add any credibility to her accusations. Heath would be furious with her if he thought anyone knew about their relationship. He had been very clear that no one was to know that they were sleeping together or that there was anything to their relationship other than her professional interest in his discoveries.

Finally, she decided she had waited long enough. She casually laid down the read outs that Bruce and Amehd had given each of them and stood. "I still have some film to develop, so unless there is anything I can do here to be of assistance, I will head back to the dark room."

No one seemed to respond, so she simply turned and left. Unfortunately Heath's disposition had not changed a great deal by the time Denise made her way back to their rooms. She entered her own bedroom but could hear him in the adjoining setting room. She wasn't looking forward to what she knew was going to be a bad situation.

"I hear you over there. Get in here." Heath demanded.

She flipped her long hair back over her shoulder and took in a deep breath to steady herself. Knowing that she couldn't avoid the impending confrontation she opened the door to the setting room.

Heath was setting in a chair with his back to the door, but she could tell from the table next to him that he had been drinking since he left the group. A nearly empty bottle of Jack Daniels was all the initial proof she needed. If she could have gotten away with it, she would have slipped back through the door and locked herself in her own room. She knew all too well how nasty Heath could be if he had been drinking for the last two hours.

"I said get in here damn you." He said again without turning to look in her direction.

"I'm coming, just give me a minute. I stayed at the meeting so that I could keep you appraised on what was discussed." Denise tried to steady her voice not to show her hesitation or fear.

"Like anything they could have had to discuss would be of any worth to me." He replied coldly. "Those fools are going to be the ruin of me if I let them keep dragging their feet. We have to find the hidden treasure in the Seven Caves to make all this pay off for us. You know that don't you?"

"Yes Heath, of course I know exactly what our objective is. I won't let you down. You know that I won't let you down." She said almost as if she were pleading for her self.

"I don't give a damn about all this esoteric bullshit. There is gold and jewels there to be found that are going to make me one of the richest men in the world and I'll be damn if I am going to let a bunch of religious historians take me off track. I've found all there is of any worth in Peru and I don't intend to be spending my time retracing my steps."

Denise stood quietly as Heath continued to vent. She didn't want to do anything to agitate him any more than the others already had. He had only hit her once, but once was enough. He was a big man and she had carried around a bruise the size of a baseball from that one experience. Not only was she not in anyway interested in a repeat of that kind of shocking pain, she knew that if anything happened to cause the rest of the group to think Heath had hit her it would only cause more trouble for them.

"Why are you standing so far away from me Denise? What, are you afraid of me just because I've had a drink or two?" Heath said sarcastically and with a bit of a slur beginning to appear in his speech.

"No, why would I be afraid of you Heath. We are partners remember. I am just here to assist you. I just don't know what it is you want of me right at this moment." Denise said with as much confidence and sincerity as she could manage. Her heart was beating far to fast and she knew that if he pulled her close to him he would immediately know that she was not being honest with him.

"What I want of you." Heath replied in a very slow attempt to reply. It wasn't slow in a way that it would have been if he were thinking about a response. Instead it was slow as if it took an effort for him to get each following word out.

She stood motionless and within a few minutes she realized that Heath had drank himself into a stooper. He had fallen asleep setting in the chair almost as the words were leaving his mouth. Denise waited, standing in complete silence for several moments longer before she felt safe to turn and quietly leave the room.

CHAPTER 19

Adam continued working on the language keys to the clay tablet until late into the night. Nothing he tried seemed to make sense. Gabriella who had joined him only an hour or so ago knew very well what the first four groupings were referring to. They were all significant portions of the Gnostic creation myth, which she of course knew well. It was apparent that the fifth grouping was referring to the place known as the Seven Caves but the real problem at this point was in trying to understand what the sixth and seventh grouping meant. The markings didn't even resemble the other wedge shaped marks. Why would the author have changed symbolisms for only the last two groupings?

"I wish I could be of more help Adam." Gabriella said. "It is quite a puzzle and I can see that it is bothering you not to be able to decipher it."

Adam dropped the pencil in his hand and stretched back in his chair. "Maybe I am just trying too hard. Or maybe it is beyond my capability."

Gabriella was not about to play into his insecurities. Instead she smiled and began telling Adam about her parents. "I wasn't very old when both my mother and father were killed in a horrible accident in China. Sometimes it is difficult for me to even remember what their faces looked like. I mean I have pictures, but sometimes I just want so badly to see their faces as I remember them through my own eyes, not as I have recently seen from a photograph. Do you know what I mean Adam?"

"Sure, I mean I haven't ever lost anyone that way and both of my parents are still living back on the farm in Indiana, but I think I can understand." Adam replied not really sure where Gabriella was going with this.

"Well, even though I have a difficult time remembering their faces, I can still hear their voices clearly deep within my heart. It isn't that I remember their voices in my mind. It is truly that I can hear their voices still and I hear them deep within my heart. Well, maybe it is like that with the sixth and seventh grouping. Instead of looking at them from the perspective of a voice you might remember in your mind, you need to try to view them from the perspective of a voice you might actually hear in your heart."

Adam could have listened to Gabriella for hours. He loved the sound of her voice and her thoughts and expressions were so beautiful, but he didn't have the slightest idea how what she had just said was going to help him figure out the sixth and seventh groupings.

Gabriella had been in her grandfather's study nearly all morning. Adam knew that he should be working on more of the tablet translations, but he just couldn't keep his mind on it. If they were going to be spending the next several weeks together, he had to tell Gabriella how he was feeling about her.

It was Friday and many of the shops and bazaars in Cairo were closed for the Sabbath. Amehd had gone to prayer and wouldn't be back to continue working with Bruce until much later in the day. Bruce thought that he would spend some time with Gabriella and their grandfather. After having had a few days to absorb all that they had told him of the real purpose of the Legacy House, he felt like he was ready to find out more. It surprised him to see Adam pacing outside the study doors.

"Are you waiting for someone Adam?" Bruce asked as he approached.

Adam looked a little startled by Bruce's question. It took him a few minutes to decide how he would respond. "Actually, I am. I was hoping to have a few minutes alone to talk with your sister this morning."

This was too good of a situation to let pass. Adam looked like a scared schoolboy getting ready to ask the most popular girl in school out on a first date. Bruce couldn't help himself as he teased Adam. "The goddess you mean don't you? Are you going to ask her to the Friday night picture shows?"

"Very funny Bruce. I bet you have never had the slightest problem asking a woman out on a date. But if you must know, that is pretty much just what I had in mind." Adam responded good heartedly. "Unless of course you object or think it is a bad idea or something." He added hesitantly.

Bruce smiled and put his arm around Adam as he replied. "No, no, I don't have any objections. Just remember she is my sister."

Bruce suddenly realized that he and Adam couldn't both have Gabriella's attention this morning. He decided silently that he would allow Adam to make his attempt and wait until latter to talk to her more about their family obligations.

"Come on Adam, she could be in there all day, I'll take you in but then you are on your own." Bruce still playfully smiling said as he pulled Adam closer to the large double doors of the study.

Gabriella was setting with both her bare feet up in the chair pouring over some ancient looking text when Bruce and Adam entered the study. The mid morning sun was streaming in the alabaster window pains causing shadows of light to dance around Gabriella's face and hair.

"Look who I found wondering around outside the doors Gabriella." Bruce said as way of introduction.

Gabriella looked up from the text and the genuine warmth of her bright smile told Bruce immediately that Adam wasn't the only one who had more than research on his mind. "Adam, it is nice to see you this morning." She said warmly.

"I hope you don't mind me hunting you down this way Gabriella." Adam jumped right out with it, "I was hoping that you might find some time to show me around Cairo this morning."

"Why Adam are you asking me out on a date?" Gabriella asked.

"Oh give the man a break sister dear. Who else is there in this group that he would want to show him around Cairo?" Bruce jumped in playfully.

"I can speak for myself Bruce." Adam responded quickly. "Yes, if you are interested than I would very much like to ask you on a date. What about it?"

Adam didn't know where he was getting his courage, but it just seemed to feel right to him. He stood looking very confident and quite attractive waiting for Gabriella's response.

"No, I have no objection what so ever. I would love to go out with you." Gabriella said simply as she closed the book and hugged her legs that were still folded up in front of her chest on the chair.

Bruce couldn't believe how easy she had made it on Adam. Not that it bothered him at all, it just surprised him that she was as taken with Adam as he was with her. He had watched men try to win the attentions of Gabriella for years, but she had just never been too terribly interested.

"Before we leave, Bruce you might be interested in some reading I was doing." Gabriella said as she unfolded her legs and stood. She picked up the book she had been looking at and handed it to Bruce. "There is a translation of a codex called the Historia Tolteca-Chichimeca in here that might be of help to us. It concerns the origins of the Mexican people. Their legends and creation myths tell of Chicomoztoc which is another name for the Seven Caves."

Adam's eyes lit up as he asked, "the Seven Caves as in one of the groupings on the clay tablets?"

"Well, that is what I am thinking. I know that both Cordie and Heath have spent a lot of time in Central and South America but I thought I would do a little research on my own and remembered the codex where

Chicomoztoc is shown as a seven-lobed cave with an entrance corridor below the Colhuacan, the Crooked Mountain." Gabriella explained.

"Alright, alright I'll read the information and give you a full report when you return. Now the two of you go on and get out of here before grandfather comes down and puts you both to work." Bruce jested as he nearly pushed both of them toward the study door.

Once the study was quiet again, Bruce set down and began reading the information Gabriella had left him with. It surprised him that it was not simply the Mexican tradition that spoke of the Seven Caves. He found that memories had been preserved among many of the tribes of the Mesoamericas regarding a single island landmass from which their ancestors came. The Quiche-Maya tribe of Guatemala told of a seven-fold cave in a text known as Popol Vuh. He read that the first people escaped from inside the earth only after the sun had fired an arrow of sunlight into the House of Mirrors, which was yet another name for the seven-fold cave.

Bruce was still reading when Felix entered the study some three hours later. He was very excited to see his grandfather, but didn't like at all the way he looked. Felix seemed pale and worn as he moved slowly toward his grandson.

"Are you feeling alright grandfather?" Bruce asked inquisitively.

Felix delayed replying until he had reached the same small table they had all set around the day they had returned to the Cairo Legacy House. "Son, I am as good as a man of 96 has any right to be."

It was very rare for Felix Smith to admit his age. Most people thought of him as being 10 or even 15 years younger than he really was. Bruce had known that his grandfather didn't want anyone focusing on his advanced years because he was concerned about someone outside the direct line trying to take over the Legacy House. He had never really understood the full implications of such until very recently.

The sudden death of he and Gabriella's father had thrown the normal cycle of inheritance off a bit. It had been tradition for generations past that the new watcher had taken over their responsibilities when they turned 40, leaving the old watcher around as a kind of mentor for several years yet. When Felix lost his only son in such a terrible accident, it pushed him into a much longer term as watcher than he had ever expected.

"Where is your sister?" Felix asked next.

"Believe it or not she and Adam are out on a date." Bruce explained.

The news brought a smile of satisfaction to Felix's tired face. "That is a good thing you know. Adam would make a good husband for that girl."

"Husband!" Bruce replied with surprise. "Aren't you rushing things just a bit grandfather?"

Felix didn't hesitate in replying, "Just you watch and see. I have a feeling about this and besides she is older now than your mother was when she married your father."

Bruce could not help but laugh lightly as he picked up the book he had been reading when Felix entered the study. He moved over to the table where the old man set and took a seat next to him. "Grandfather, can you tell me about the book that you had on the table here when we spoke about the true purpose of the Legacy House?" he asked with sincere respect.

"Yes son, we should talk of that. I guess it would be alright to do so without Gabriella. Go to the last shelves of books there on the end. Push in the small button on the bottom edge of the second shelf." Felix instructed.

Without question Bruce did as his grandfather had instructed. The shelf pivoted to reveal a hidden chamber with its own shelf behind the front façade. There he saw the same ancient looking book that had been lying on the table. He carefully reached in and pulled the book out. He had almost expected to feel some kind of energy or power emanating from the book as he had from his grandfather and sister's hands. He did not however; it just felt like any other very old, quite heavy book. Holding it gingerly in both his hands he walked back and laid the book down in front of his grandfather.

"This son is the oldest record of our genealogy. The record of our family line all the way back to Seth, the son of Adam and Eve. It explains how Ialdabaoth took power from his mother Wisdom upon his creation, much the same as it is explained in *The Secret Book According to John*. It goes on to explain how the efforts of Wisdom, aided by higher aeons of the spiritual universe to regain the stolen power leads to Ialdabaoth surrendering the power into successive generation of the human race. It is then that Ialdabaoth and his offspring enslave humankind by creating destiny and the physical body as a prison for the soul. It clearly lays out the three groups of the human race; our own line, the posterity of Seth, secondly the posterity of Noah, which included the descendants of Shem, Ham, and Japheth, and finally the third group who are the apostates from the descendants of Ham and Japheth who join the posterity of Seth and come under their protection.

This is important son, because I believe that both Adam and Cordie's ancestors would be found in this third group. I cannot be completely sure you understand, but I have strong feelings that I am right on this issue.

Once you have read and understand the teachings of this book son, you will have a good understanding of the interior mystical journey of the soul to acquaintance with the ineffable first principle, God. The last portion of the book records sacred hymns of our people. They express desire for acquaintance and then thanksgiving for the receipt of acquaintance that you should make yourself familiar with."

When Felix finished talking he simply stood up and slowly walked toward the large double doors of the study. He paused only briefly before opening the doors. "Be sure to replace the book when you are finished son."

CHAPTER 20

Adam and Gabriella had had a wonderful day together. Neither could explain the strange feeling of familiarity that they seemed to already share. They seemed to almost know things about each other on an unconscious level that they couldn't really bring into the forefront of their minds, yet still did exist. It was almost as if they somehow knew instinctively little things about each other. Things that neither were really aware of, but that both felt very deeply in their souls. A bond was definitely forming between them.

Adam had to force himself to suggest that they end their date and they had just made it back to the Legacy House in time to join the assembled group for the late afternoon meal. Adam felt a little guilty knowing that he was not going to have anything new to report on the meanings of the sixth or seventh grouping, but he wouldn't have traded his morning with Gabriella for anything.

Felix was already seated when the young couple entered the dinning room. Gabriella went straight to him and leaned down to softly kiss him on the cheek. She had had such a pleasant morning and she somehow knew her grandfather was to thank for it. She also wanted to get a look at him up close. She had not liked how tired and worn out he had been looking the last few days.

"Good afternoon dear." Felix said with a smile. "You look bright and shinny this afternoon."

Adam didn't know just exactly what it was, but something in Felix's greeting to his granddaughter cause a bell of recognition to go off in his mind. He quickly pulled his small scratch notepad out of his pants pocket and opened it to some of the original scratches he had made after first seeing the clay tablets. His mind was racing as he flipped through the previous pages of his notebook.

It was Cordie who noticed Adam's excitement and moved closer to him. She watched for a moment and having seen that look in his eye many time as they had worked together on a student problem or issue for the class she encouraged him to share what he was thinking. "Adam, I know that look. What is it? Have you had a break through?"

Adam looked up from his notebook with a bright smile beaming from his handsome face. "I am not sure it is a break through, but yes I think I am on to something." Look at these markings here Cordie. Couldn't this be spelling out the word Diva?" Then here right beside it would be Ati."

Felix stood with the anticipation of what Adam was about to reveal. From the end of the table he seemed to make the connection and surprisingly came to the realization that the text had taken a turn toward the teachings of Buddha. He said very calmly but with a fare amount of confidence, "The Shining One just like the shining ones in the book of Enoch. In Buddha teachings Diva represents the shining one or one of the inhabitants of one of the good modes of existence who live in fortunate realms of the heavens but who, like other beings are subject to the cycle of rebirth; where as Ati means great perfection. Ati is the primary teaching of the Nyingmapa school of Tibetan Buddhism."

"Felix, I am a little rusty on my Buddhist history but isn't Ati considered the definitive and most secret teaching of Shakyamuni Buddha?" Cordie asked.

"Yes, you are not too rusty it seems." Felix replied. "It is complicated to explain but it teaches that purity of mind is always present and needs only to be recognized."

"But what does Buddhist teaching have to do with the other group-ings on the tablet?" Adam asked puzzled at his own discovery. "That is what was blocking my understanding, I wasn't looking for Buddhist ter-minology."

Bruce was beginning to understand a great deal more about the sig-nificance of these shinning ones, no matter what religion spoke of them. He wasn't sure what to say, and felt a bit of relief when Cordie responded to Adam's confusion.

"Maybe a broader understanding of religions of the world is needed here, just as we prescribe it to our students in our own class Adam." Cordie reminded Adam of what he already knew.

He immediately replayed Cordie's opening comments from the Understanding Religion portion of their class in his mind.

Religion can be defined as simply as saying that it is a noun meaning faith or belief. For my purposes I will take it a bit further and identify religion as *mankind's faith, beliefs, emotions, behaviors and/or attitudes about our own relationship with the powers of the universe as created by God.* Our look at religion will include spiritual traditions and philoso-phies that may be historically significant, explanatory of indigenous traditions and have a link to our better understanding of our begin-nings as God provided. The beliefs sometimes referred to, as Creation Myths within these religions will be especially significant.

Beginning with The Bahá'í Faith of Iran in which there is only one God and that God is actively concerned about the development of humanity we see one of the many religions that centers on God and his desire to teach humanity in relationship to morals and social values. The God of the Bahá'í Faith is the same one and only God of the Christian, Islamic, Jewish, and Zoroastrianism faith. The Bahá'í Faith teaches that God sends messengers to aid humans in learning his les-sons and to understand the "oneness of humanity", which is that all humans come from the same original stock and deserve equal opportu-nities and treatment. Many of these messengers include, Abraham,

Moses, Zoroaster, Krishna, Buddha, Muhammad and Jesus. The origin and time of origin of that one original stock is the focus of our search.

The earliest dates attributed to a monotheistic religion are said to be between 2000 to 1800 B.C.E. with the founding of Zoroastrianism. The Eastern Iranian worship of *Ahura Mazda,* The Wise Lord was the belief in the One Supreme, Omnipotent, and Omniscient God. By 650 A.D. there were literally millions of Zoroastrians worshiping God.

All of the sudden a link between the supposed Christian or Jewish character of Enoch, the references to the Gnostic creation myth and elements of Buddhism all being found on one ancient clay tablet didn't seem so far fetched. He didn't know if it had been Gabriella telling him to look where he did not first expect to find the answer, or Felix's mention of how shinny Gabriella looked, but Adam was sure that he would now be able to also figure out the seventh grouping as long as he applied the same broad perspective to it.

The afternoon meal was served and everyone ate with a look of pleasure on their faces. It could have of course been because of the excellent culinary skill of Jamila, but Adam also thought that it had something to do with his most recent success.

It was Heath who spoke up immediately after Felix had signaled for the meeting to begin. "I want to apologize for my rash behavior over the Peru discussion. Now having done so, I would like to point out that I still do not believe anything that we have found is pointing us in the direction of any of the mentioned Peruvian locations. I believe our next step is to make some decisions about where we believe the Island of the Seven Caves is located, just as we did with the crystal chamber. Once we have that list we should evaluate them just as we did the possibilities of the location for the crystal chamber and set out to find them one by one, until we are successful, as we were on our first attempt with the crystal chamber."

No one could argue with his rational, but as always it just seemed that Heath Conrad was pushing to rush into something before it was completely thought out.

Felix eventually agreed and told the group to work in two groups of three each to make up the list. He was not including himself nor Adam in the teams as they would continue to work on translating the seventh grouping.

CHAPTER 21

The jet was loaded and everyone was on board. The same long conference table that had seemed so large when it was just Adam, Bruce and Cordie now seemed crowded. Gabriella had taken her position at the opposite end of the table as her grandfather, though she still wondered if Bruce should not be occupying her position. It wasn't that she didn't feel capable or worthy of the role of Watcher, it was just that she had seen her brother learn and take in great understanding and mastery of teachings, in just a few days, that had taken her years to achieve. She wondered if her being born first had somehow been a mistake.

Heath set directly across the table from Cordie with only Denise seated as a buffer between himself and Amehd. He wished the computer monitors did not so completely block his vision of Cordie. He had not had much time at all to be around her and it was beginning to distract him. He needed to keep his mind on the mission at hand. There wasn't any good reason for him to keep remembering those days so many years ago when they were together. He had to keep his mind on finding the correct location of the Seven Caves.

Everyone had finally given in to Heath's strong-arming and agreed that the next step was to try to find an antediluvian civilization reaching back into the mesmerizing mists of time, called in may parts of the world, The Seven Caves. Doing such fell squarely on the broad shoulders of Heath. He knew as much, and so did the other seven members of the expedition. He knew very well that if his suspicions were right, he would be taking the group into lands of which tourist never ventured. The comforts of the Legacy House jet would seem luxurious compared to the mosquito-infested military controlled area of a nearly forgotten little swampy island near Cuba.

"Have we gotten government permission to fly directly into the Isle of Youth?" Heath finally asked out loud.

"Yes, it took some doing but the proper permits were issued and faxed to me just prior to our leaving the Legacy House. We are cleared to bypass Havana and fly directly into Nueva Gerona airport." Felix responded dryly.

Gabriella was worried. Even Jamila had noticed before they left the house that her grandfather seemed tired and run down all of the sudden. Felix was an old man, but to Gabriella he was her strong enduring grandfather and she could not imagine life without him. She didn't say anything, but instead watched Felix attentively.

Felix had all of the proper paperwork and permits to allow the group to pass through the army checkpoint and drive the land rovers in as far as possible. Once the vehicles could go no further, Heath took up the lead. There was an almost boyish look of excitement in his eyes and he headed out on foot. Gabriella and Bruce followed behind their grandfather with feelings of trepidation. Not knowing how far they would have to make it on foot, they both feared for the health of Felix who was still looking older and more worn than either of them had ever remembered.

Adam followed immediately behind Gabriella with Cordie next to him. It was Amehd and Denise who made up the rear. Cordie had noticed Adam's interest in Gabriella and took the opportunity to express her approval. She had not had a great deal of time to spend alone with Adam since their whole adventure had begun. It felt comforting to be laughing with him in such an easy manner once again.

Suddenly Heath threw up his arm signaling for everyone to freeze. The effect was like that of a row of dominoes, but within seconds everyone was silent and standing as still as a statue. The harsh late morning sun was beating down on the group as eerie black and white vultures circled overhead in gliding patterns of attack.

Heath pointed down toward a large patch of shrubs. "We are entering a hazardous swampland that is going to lead us to a flight of steps just beyond a derelict telecommunications station. The entire area between here and there is going to be heavy with these particular shrubs. They are poisonous and must be avoided. We don't have any antidote for them, so pay very close attention to where you are walking from this point on."

The group continued at a much more cautious rate toward the southeast corner of the island. There was no sign of life in the run down telecom station and the group found themselves at the flight of steps Heath had told them to expect. Moving down the worn and unattended stone steps they found themselves entering a lower level of sandy swampland. Denise was already busy with her camera, taking pictures of the large crocodiles and the Cuban sandhill crane just off to the right of the group.

Adam lunged forward and grabbed Gabriella just as she was about to step into a large pocket of sand crabs. They wouldn't have been deadly by any means but their attach might have been quite uncomfortable. He pointed down and Gabriella smiled in appreciation as they continued still not speaking.

As they finally reached the slightly raised ground of a low cliff face, Heath increased his pace. He was almost in a run as he entered the thick tree coverage just ahead of them. He could feel his heartbeat quickening with anticipation. Felix was breathing a little heavier than Bruce would have liked, but otherwise he seemed to be holding up pretty well.

"Here, we have found Cueva #1." Heath's voice sounded back to the group. Adam and Gabriella moved forward to join Heath who was still running his fingers over the metal plaque on the right-hand side of the cave entrance.

"I'll get the rest of the team before we enter." Adam said as he turned to go back and retrieve everyone else. He didn't have far to go, everyone had already begun the slight climb through the trees to the cave entrance.

It was all Heath could do to hold himself back until the others had joined him. He was sure that they had reached the original site of the Seven Caves and he knew it was a discovery that could not be matched by any of his previous finds.

Gabriella and Bruce both felt some unseen force pulling them toward the cave entrance. They looked at each other and without exchanging a word knew that the other was feeling the same strange calling to enter the cave. While Heath believed he was on the path of a great historical and archaeological find of great value, it was only Gabriella, Bruce and their grandfather that had any idea that the answers to the world's greatest mystery surely lied inside one of the caves of this island.

Standing in the clearing beyond the tree coverage all eight of the group looked up at the gaping mouth of the large open cave, Punta del Este's Cueva #1. Heath's confidence was balanced by Felix's wisdom as he finally spoke. "Are we ready to put our theories to the test? Lets proceed with extreme caution, we do not want to contaminate the site in any way that might jeopardize finding the proper resting place of the crystals."

As they moved slowly into the unwelcoming interior of the cave, Bruce noticed just how normal the cave was for this part of the world. Although it was a relief to be out of the beating down rays of the harsh sun of the island, the immediate interior seemed to be nothing more than a home for countless numbers of bats and mosquitoes. The ammonia smell of the piled up bad droppings nearly caused the group to gage and choke as they moved further into the cave.

Then just a few steps further into the cave, as their eyes adjusted to the darker interior, Gabriella saw the astonishing faded red and black petroglyphs composing a whole series of rings and geometric forms. At the same time Amehd was attracted to the overhead skylights. Having studied the stars it seemed only natural to him that he would first notice the two roughly circular openings cut through the soft rock by ancient hands. Being still the early part of the day, sunlight filtered down through the openings, but Amehd could imagine watching the lights of the sky through them at night.

Bruce was examining the broken pieces of conch shell that covered much of the cave flooring. He knew most likely it had been discarded hundreds of years ago by Amerindians who either occupied or made pilgrimages to the cave.

CHAPTER 22

The entire group had been so taken by the marvelous finds within the cave. It was Heath though who was immediately searching for the proper locations for the crystals. They didn't have a lot to go on. They only knew that all three of the crystals must be placed in the proper lock for them to work as keys. He knew that more than likely a stone dais had once stood under the forward skylight and so began his first in depth search for a lock in that area.

"We are going to have to set up lights." Bruce announced. "We have been exploring for some time and the afternoon sun is beginning to diminish. If we want to continue our efforts we are going to need lighting."

"Yes son, that is a fine idea. If you can organize that I will begin to lay our search grids for each of us to cover in groups of two." Felix commented.

It was Denise that brought up the idea of eating, which when mentioned sounded like a good idea to everyone. While Bruce and Heath began setting up the lighting Gabriella and Cordie started unpacking a large picnic basket that they had brought with them from the plane. They had survival supplies that would last for days if need be, but it was nice to have fresh sandwiches, fruit and chilled bean salad for this first meal in the cave. As always Jamila had taken great care in packing a fine meal for them.

Felix handled the pause for their dinner just as he had the large afternoon meals in Cairo. As soon as it looked as if everyone was finishing, he began the customary meeting. He reviewed the group and grid assignments he had earlier announced and made sure everyone knew that above all else, they were looking for the three locks where the crystal keys were to be placed.

With the soft yellow light of the artificial lanterns the entire cave became visible. Denise was taking photographs but it was Cordie and Gabriella who seemed most interested in studding the largest most dramatic drawing on the main chamber wall.

Cordie traced her finger lightly over each of the 50 to 55 concentric circles making up the drawing. They alternated between the charcoal black coloring and the ochre red. There was no doubt about the clear resemblance of the drawing to a bulls' eye or target. There was also a long arrow like stick drawn from the center to the outer ring, very much like an arrow piercing the center of the target. In all it was a huge multi-faceted petroglyph that seemed to have enormous significance within the large 12 to 15 meter central cavern.

Amhed and Adam had been assigned a grid taking them down the clearly man made corridor off to the right of the main chamber. It was about 10 meters long so they carried a hand held light to make their task a little easier. It was strange in deed that the corridor didn't seem to lead anywhere in particular. They found a very interesting symbol that looked very much like a cross formed out of gradually unwinding concentric rings, but nothing that looked like a resting place for the crystals.

Heath had been allowed to continue his efforts with the assistance of Denise in examining the grid of the area under the front skylight. He felt sure that at least one of the crystal keys should fit in a lock somewhere in that area.

The only problem with the lighting, was that it also attracted swarms of insects. They had all been covered with repellant and their clothing had even been soaked in a type of anti-insect treatment, but this was known as one of the worst spots on the island for insects. After hours of putting up with them and covering every centimeter of their assigned grids, it was agreed to take a break and turn down the lights.

Once the artificial lights had been dampened a remarkable thing began to happen. The light of the predawn began to shine in through the two skylights. The group had worked through the whole of the night without really realizing it. Unfortunately they had worked through the whole of the night also without having found even the first lock for the crystal keys.

As the sun rose and the sky lightened above the cave opening the most beautiful rays of pink and lavender light began to filter down into the cave from both skylights. It hit everyone's minds almost instantly that the colors of the sunrays dancing into the cave and filtering slowly down in visible rays of transparency mixed with a mystical element resembled the same soft pink and lavender colors emanating from the crystals when they entered the crystal chamber in Egypt.

It only lasted for a few brief minutes but it had been enough to give the group the encouragement that they needed to continue the search. There had to be a connection between this cave and the crystals.

Felix asked for some fresh water and moved over near the entrance to one of the seven lobed caverns that expanded off the main chamber of the cave. He slowly set down and began thinking. After several minutes he very slowly and in a deliberate tone asked, "Cordie can you tell us all again the mythology of the Seven Caves?"

Cordie turned and wiped her dirty hand across her face leaving a streak of the dust she had been crawling in on her face. "Sure, Chicomoztoc, beneath Colhuocan or the crooked mountain was the birth place of human kind. A lightning staff was struck on the Seven Caves to begin the process. Another version describes the escape of human kind from inside the earth only after the sun had fired an arrow of sunlight into the House of Mirrors or otherwise known as the seven-fold cave."

Bruce watched the look of frustration and discouragement on his grandfather's face as Cordie recounted the tales. He waited patiently to hear what his grandfather had discovered.

Shaking his head and almost looking as angry as he had the day he slammed his fist on the table of the dinning room in Cairo Felix finally revealed in a harsh voice what no one else had caught onto yet. "We have made a critical error. We won't find the answers we need here, until we are able to find and bring the Golden Wedge of Cuzco here to the Seven Caves."

Heath pulled his ball cap from atop his dark curls and flung it furiously against the floor of the cave. He had been right, he was sure about this being the Seven Caves, but his haste and determination had caused him to persuade the entire group to by pass a trip, which he had thought useless to Cuzco in Peru.

"Felix, of course," Cordie said, "The Golden Wedge is also referred to as the Golden Arrow and could be the lightning staff that was struck on the Seven Caves. Do you think it really exists?"

"Of course it really exists." Felix replied with confidence. "The crystals existed and we found them didn't we. Now we are going to have to find the Golden Wedge before we are able to make the crystals work. I would be willing to bet that on the equinoxes a beam of sunlight penetrates this cave from the forward skylight. That beam of sunlight would slowly cross from the center of the target symbol to the edge via the arrow like image. That was the reminder of the power of the cave. But with the Golden Wedge the early morning pre dawn sun rays of soft pink and lavender will actually activate the crystals to open the power of the cave. It is all so clear now. You'll have to go to Peru immediately."

Bruce and Gabriella shot a shocked look at each other. They had both heard what their grandfather had said, you will have to go to Peru, rather than we will have to go to Peru.

Bruce verbalized he and Gabriella's fears. "What do you mean grandfather? Who will need to go to Peru?"

"Everyone with the exception of myself, Gabriella and Adam." The old man replied without hesitation.

"What, you expect us to leave the three of you in this bug infested cave for who knows how long as the rest of us just hop back on the jet and fly off to Peru!" Bruce protested.

"There is a lot of work to be done here, but I think the three of us should be able to handle it on our own. We have ample supplies and there is little real danger here. Besides if we get too tired of living in the cave, we can always find a way into that old communication building down the grotto. No, I am sure this is the best solution." Felix replied firmly.

"I would like to speak with you privately as the others hike back to the land rovers and bring the other supplies needed for a week or so stay." Felix said to Bruce.

Everyone else still stood looking a little bewildered at each other until Bruce finally agreed and sent them off on the hike back to the land rovers.

Felix remained seated leaning back against the stone of the cave wall. He waited until he could no longer hear any of the others making their way back out past the bats and into the open.

"Bruce, come over here and set with me son." His voice was weak and frail sounding. "I have hidden my weariness from the others but you need to realize that I could not make the trip to Peru even if I wished to. I am an old man Bruce. I have known that my time was coming for sometime now. I will not leave this cave. At least not in the same way I entered it."

"Grandfather, what are you talking about?" Bruce asked franticly. He felt like the same frightened young boy who had to listen to his grandfather tell him that he had lost both his parents all those years ago.

Felix lifted his hand and placed it on Bruce's arm as he comforted him by adding, "I am not going to die this minute son. In fact I am probably not going to die for some time, but I could never make that climb up to Machu Picchu. You know I will be better off here with your sister and young Adam. Now here is what I need you to make sure happens in Cuzco."

They had plenty of time to talk over Felix's concerns about sending Heath out with Cordie and Amehd and just how important it was that the Golden Wedge be retrieved if they were to complete their exploration. In fact, by the time they heard the others returning with the supplies they had moved on to talk about Felix's plan for Gabriella and Adam.

CHAPTER 23

Bruce didn't like leaving his grandfather behind, but he knew that it was his only option. Felix had been right, they couldn't leave this in the hands of Heath Conrad and Cordie alone might not be strong enough to stand up to him if something went wrong. Even if nothing went wrong and they had the best of luck, they would have to be gone at least four or five days. They could only fly the Legacy House jet in as far as Cuzco, if they were required to go on up to Machu Picchu, which Bruce had the strongest feeling that they would, they would have to take the tourist train. To try to hire a helicopter would draw too much attention to them.

They had left more than enough fresh water and supplies for the three of them left at the cave. It still just didn't feel right to be flying off the island knowing that his sister, grandfather and Adam were left behind.

"It will not be a long flight across the continent to Peru." Amehd pointed out. "We should all probably try to get some rest."

Heath said nothing but shot a contemptuous look across the conference table to where Amehd stood. It still aggravated Heath that such a small little man as Amehd had been right and that they should have gone to Cuzco prior to ever setting out to find the Seven Caves. He didn't like being wrong, but he especially didn't like being outdone by academics that didn't have a fraction of the field experience that he did.

"I think that sounds like a good idea. I'll be in my cabin if anyone needs me." Cordie replied and turned to leave the main conference area.

Bruce said nothing as he watched the others and wondered about how his grandfather was getting along. He knew that Gabriella would take good care of him, but he also knew that Felix was a great deal weaker than he had been willing to admit.

As soon as the jet had landed at Cuzco's Aeropuerto Velasco Astete, Bruce arranged for a local driver to take them the 2 miles on into the city of Cuzco. They had agreed to go straight to the Palacio del Almirante and tour the Museo Arqueologico. The car took them along Cuesta del Almmirante Street directly to the beautiful colonial mansion, which housed the museum. Cordie had done a great deal of work in the museum when she was still with the Vatican and knew she would be well received by the local archeologists and scientist there.

While she was trying to get some leads from old acquaintances the rest of the group would go ahead to the Temple of the Sun. Heath was sure that their trip to the temple would be a waste of time. He believed now that they would have to travel to Machu Picchu to find an entrance to a series of underground passages that he hoped just as in Cairo would lead then on the same path as he had practiced in Scotland. That was the only thing that made any sense to him but he wasn't going to push too hard. After all, it was his pushing too hard that had caused them to miss this step altogether in the first place.

Of course in Heath's eyes all he saw when he looked out over the Coricancha church that now stood built over the ruins of the Temple of the Sun were the fabled life-size gold and silver statues of plants and animals that had once stood in the terraces around the temple site. He had seen and explored the mortarless masonry and earthquake proof trapezoidal doorways of the temple, but he knew that by the others seeing it for themselves, they would be more likely to believe in his theory of these people having had the same capability to construct such an elaborate labyrinth as they had already seen in both Scotland and Egypt.

Cordie never did show up at the Temple of the Sun. They had all agreed that if they didn't reconnect at the temple, they would meet at the hotel they were going to spend the night in. By the time the group entered the lobby of the Hotel El Dorado, Cordie was already setting in front of the fireplace enjoying a coca tea.

"Well, what do you think Cordie? Was your trip to the museum of any help?" Bruce asked casually as he sat down to join her.

"It very well may have been." Cordie had greatly enjoyed seeing so many of her old friends at the museum and listening to their still passionate love of their local history had in a way reenergized her. She had not allowed herself to remember how happy she had been during her lifetime in South America because having done so would have also required her remembering her life with Heath. In order to purge him from her mind and heart Cordie was beginning to realize that she had shut off a great deal more of herself and her past than she had previously realized. "I think we should all have a good meal, a good night's sleep and catch the tourist train to Machu Picchu just as Heath had originally thought." Cordie added confidently. "Has anyone thought about where we should have dinner this evening?"

"What about Le Tetama?" Heath replied.

Cordie knew that Heath must have remembered that Le Tetama was one of her favorite restaurants in all of South America. They had eaten there together many times. She wondered what his motivations for suggesting it had been, but at the same time liked the idea of dinning there again. "They probably even still have their nightly folk music show that Denise and the others who have never visited Peru might really enjoy. I think that is a good idea. Does everyone else agree?" she finally replied not wanting to give Heath too much credit for the original suggestion.

Denise and Cordie were sharing a room with vaulted brick ceilings, curving walls and lovely alpaca-skin bedcovers. They both enjoyed the hot showers and then changed for dinner without saying too much of anything to each other. Cordie wondered why Denise was even making the attempt to keep up such pretence instead of sharing a room with Heath, but she kept her thoughts to herself.

The men were waiting for them in the hotel lobby and they all headed out to Le Retama. It was a cool evening as they walked along the long steep cobblestone streets. Cordie couldn't help but remember all of the very happy nights she and Heath had spent walking along these same streets. She did everything she could to suppress the memories and focus on the present.

It became much easier as they were seated for dinner. Bruce asked what she or Heath might recommend from the menu. Cordie had suggested the trout in fennel cream sauce still one of the house specialties. Heath on the other hand, mischievously suggested the cuy. It was all Cordie could do as Denise took up Heath's suggestion and ordered the cuy, not to tell the poor fool that she was asking for a local delicacy better know as guinea pig. The look on Denise's face when the plate was set in front of her with the whole guinea pig resting in a pool of hot sauce, proved to be worth her silence.

The restaurant was noisy enough that the group felt comfortable talking freely about what Cordie believed she had found from her visit to the museum.

"All indications point to the mystical city of Machu Picchu." she began to say. "From what we know about the item we are looking for, it is probably located underground somewhere between Machu Picchu and here. The evidence of Machu Picchu having been such a mystical place links it even more so to the Giza site so I think we look for a similar way into an underground labyrinth. What about you guys? Did you come up with anything at the temple?"

Nothing made Heath any happier than to hear Cordie supporting his ideas. Still he remained quiet as Amehd explained that although they had marveled at the stone construction he for one did not believe they discovered anything of use.

Gabriella and Adam had spent the remainder of the day clearing the mound of dirt that had built up beneath the back skylight of the cave. Felix had studied several of the pictures along the corridor earlier in the day, but as the evening began to fall he had unrolled one of the well padded sleeping bags and laid down for a short nap. He was still sleeping comfortably when Gabriella had finished preparing their dinner.

"Do you think I should wake him to eat?" Adam asked as he finished washing his hands. "It looks like you have prepared us quite a meal here. I would hate for Felix to miss it."

Gabriella smiled at Adam and then looked back down at the simple soup she had warmed. It was far from anything to brag about, but for preparing it in a cave she supposed it wasn't too bad. The strangest sensation overtook Gabriella as she continued to stir the warm soup. For just a moment it was as if she had set stirring a pot of soup in this same primitive fashion at some very distant point in time. Then just as quickly as it had overtaken her, the sensation was gone.

After pulling herself back to the moment and some thought on the question, Gabriella replied, "Yes I think we should try to wake him while the soup is still hot. Don't you think so?"

Adam liked the way that Gabriella was capable of making decisions yet open enough to ask for his opinion as well. He moved over to where Felix lied and began to gently shake the old man's shoulder.

"Gabriella has warmed us some fine smelling soup." Adam said as Felix began to wake.

Felix could not believe that he had slept as long as he had nor could he believe how much progress Adam and his granddaughter had made in clearing out the rubble of time that had built up in the cave. He felt much stronger again after having such a rest and was happy to join the young couple around the fire for a meal.

The soup was hot and nourishing. Gabriella had done a good job. Adam had also done a good job clearing the mound under the back skylight. Felix felt very fortunate to have both of them here with him. He realized that he would soon need to begin preparing Adam for what was ahead of them, but not tonight. Tonight would be a time to just enjoy each others company and watch the movement of the stars as they appeared above the two sky lights.

CHAPTER 24

As Cordie slept she was tormented with dreams of vivid reality. All night long it had seemed old memories and behaviors gnawed away at her sleeping mind. The dreams were relentless in their attempts to pull her back into the torment of her past life with Heath. She tossed and turned in the small bed while the destructive power of her love for a man who's values and ways were so out of alignment with her own painted a hideously grotesque portrait of her youth.

Then just before she woke, she saw Denise in place of herself. Denise was nearly the same age now that Cordie had been when she had allowed Heath to pull her into his world. For that last few minutes of dreaming state just before the dream completely fades and one awakes, Cordie was beginning to understand that she had such a strong mixture of both jealousy and pity towards Denise. But then it was gone.

By the time Cordie woke, Denise had already left the room. It didn't surprise Cordie to find her in the hotel café with Heath. What did surprise her was that Amehd was with them and Heath was explaining Machu Picchu to them both.

"The Machu Picchu archaeological complex is located in the department of Cusco, in the Urubamba province and district of Machu Picchu. It is perched on the eastern slopes of the Vilcanota mountain range, a chain of mountains curtailed by the Apurimac and Urubamba

Rivers. Machu Picchu is located at a height of 2,350 meters above sea level." Codie overheard Heath explaining.

"It sounds as if you could write your own tour book or travel article." Cordie said sarcastically as she moved in to join them at their breakfast table.

Amehd stood with his palms up as Cordie took her seat, but Heath just reached for the jam and looked agitated at her comment. Bruce was not down yet either, but they still had plenty of time to reach the train.

"I had asked Heath to give me some general background information." Denise said pleasantly enough.

"I am sure he was eager to help." Cordie volleyed back toward the young woman. "How about us talking about what is really important. How are we going to find the entrance to the underground tunnels?"

Heath uncomfortably looked around the café to make sure no one else was listening to their conversation. Seeing that the café was nearly empty he responded quietly, "I think it would be best to divide up into two groups to explore the primary structures while the tourists are around. Once the majority of them have left to catch the train back down here to Cuzco we can meet up and decide just where we want to dig."

"Dig" Cordie responded with surprise. "We don't have any dig permits and I don't think it is going to be necessary to dig our way in."

"We don't have time to worry about dig permits." Heath replied sharply. "Besides you know as well as I do we would never be able to get one approved. And what do you mean you don't think digging will be necessary? Do you think there is just some entrance to underground tunneling that no one has stumbled upon somewhere up there in the open?"

Cordie glared back at Heath. They had both been all over the complex and he knew as well as she did that no submerged chambers had ever been detected. "No, you know very well that was not what I meant." was all that she could respond with.

"What did you mean Cordie?" Amehd asked very politely. "Do you have an idea about finding the entrance?"

Cordie realized she was letting Heath get to her again. She turned her attention to Amehd and calmed herself before replying. "No, not really I just feel like if it is meant for us to find the Golden Wedge we will find it. If finding it means excavating within the Machu Picchu complex then I don't believe it is meant for us to find it."

"What in the hell are you talking about? Not meant to be! What kind of spiritual mambo gumbo talk is that?" Heath replied in discussed. "Now I remember why I let you go in the first place."

Cordie couldn't contain herself. She jumped to a standing position, looked angrily back toward Heath and yelled. "Let me go! There wasn't a thing in the world that you could have done to stop me from leaving. I just can't believe I stayed with you as long as I did!"

Bruce had just entered the café and couldn't believe the scene unfolding before his eyes. Cordie was red in the face and looked as if she could actually kill Heath. He didn't have much time to react; the café staff was already informing the hotel management of the commotion. What would Felix do to handle this?

Heath let out a arrogant laugh as if Cordie's response had been entertaining to him which only seemed to infuriate Cordie even more so. Denise set speechless and Amehd was just beginning to stand and say something to comfort Cordie. Bruce knew he had to act and act now.

"Cordelia Emrys, I can't believe my good fortune." Bruce shouted out as if he were playing a role in some odd drama. "I am so excited to run into you Doctor Emrys. Would this be a good time for us to talk about….."

Cordie didn't have the slightest idea of what Bruce was talking about. She looked at him puzzled and confused. He cautiously pointed over his shoulder at the café staff and manager of the hotel coming in toward them.

Cordie realized that she was making a scene and that Bruce was trying to pull her away from Heath and the table so that he could calm her down. Her anger was immediately replaced with embarrassment. All she could do was lower her face and follow Bruce from the café.

Once they had made their way through the hotel lobby and past the inquisitive eyes of the hotel manager Bruce took a gentle hold of Cordie's arm. He led her a few paces down the stone walling beside the hotel and then finally asked, "Are you alright?"

Cordie looked up at Bruce with the start of tears swelling up in her otherwise lovely blue eyes. "Why does that man still get to me?" she pleaded.

Bruce wished more than ever that he had stayed at the cave and Felix were here to handle this. He wanted to say something that would help, but he simply didn't have the slightest clue as to what that would be. Instead he just reached out and put his arms around Cordie who was now trembling.

Amehd gave them a few minutes alone before he joined them outside the hotel. "Should we proceeded toward the train station?" he asked cautiously.

Cordie lifted her head from Bruce's chest and turned to look toward Amehd's voice. She forced a bit of a smile, straightened her shoulders and replied, "Yes Amehd I believe that is the best idea I have heard yet this morning. Unfortunately I imagine when you say we, that still includes Heath and Denise?"

The startled look on Amehd's face caused Bruce to laugh which in turn freed Cordie up to laugh just a bit herself.

"Don't worry Amehd. I was only joking. Despite my most recent outbursts that might lead you to believe differently, I can handle Heath Conrad. Let's go, we need to catch that train." Cordie said sounding more like her self.

Denise and Heath entered the train and took their seats a few rows in front of where Cordie, Bruce and Amehd already sat. Bruce was relieved to see that at least Heath had used the good sense not to push Cordie any further. He was also relieved that there wasn't too large of a crowd on the tourist train. It was late in the season and they were just catching a break Bruce told himself. It would be a lot easier on them if there weren't too many around the complex as they were looking for some sign of an entrance to the underground tunnels.

Cordie set quietly looking out the window of the train as it jerked out of the station and began the slow climb up the steep sides of the valley of Cuzco. The surroundings were so beautiful and timeless. It had been years but nothing seemed to have changes since the last time she had set out along this same journey. She watched as they chugged along past pisonayes, q'eofias, alisos, puya palm trees, and ferns, ferns of every variety known. She liked the fern best of all and they just seemed to flourish all along the valley of Cuzco.

Before she knew it they had reached the end of the lower horizontal tract of the Z shaped line and were beginning to move backwards up the oblique. It was about then that in the past she had always allowed the rocking motion of the train to lull her asleep. Of course in those days it had been Heath's firm chest that she rested her head against. Today she rested her head against the cold, dirty glass of the train window watching the distant slopes canopied in fir trees and exotic eucalyptus. The mid morning sun was bright and even seemed to warm the far off peaks of jagged mountain ranges covered in white snow.

Bruce was still concerned about Cordie, but he too was completely intoxicated by what was happening outside the train window. To his left he could see the Urabamba river swollen with dark flowing water. He knew that the Urubamba was a tributary of the Amazon and had been sacred to the ancients of the area. He pulled off his outer sweatshirt as they descended into the low-lying valley and the air temperature warmed up noticeably. He knew that they were entering an area with its own tropical micro-climate and was glad he had dressed for it.

The train was finally pulling into the Machu Piccu Puentas Ruinas station. It had been a three hour journey that had passed like a moving

picture show of the incredible mystic beauty of the surrounding land-
scape. The butterflies were thick as the group moved from the train to a
group of minibuses waiting to take them the remaining 8 kilometers up
to the Tourist Hotel.

All five of the group stood outside the hotel at the start of the path
that would lead them from the control entrance up to the citadel and
entire Machu Picchu complex.

Cordie refused to look at Heath directly but other than that Bruce
thought everything was going well. Very soon now they would be in the
cloud covered mysterious lost city of Machu Picchu.

As a group they enters the citadel in the section that housed a cluster
of rooms near the outer wall. They didn't hesitate and followed the path
through a terrace that led them through an agricultural zone before
delivering them at the opening of the urban area.

"Amehd I would like you to follow Heath and Denise on down to the
Tomb area. Cordie and I will begin with The Temple of the Sun. We can
meet up in about 4 hours to regroup and divide up what ever is remaining to be searched." Bruce said quietly.

Heath didn't like taking orders from anyone or being stuck with
Amehd trailing after he and Denise, but he didn't say anything. Amehd
didn't particularly like it any better than Heath did, but he was not
accustom to questioning orders given by who ever was designated as the
leader. Cordie took the opportunity to speak up in an effort to show
Heath that she was back in control of her emotions.

"We should be especially careful to inspect the doors. Doors are common through out the complex but especially in this sector. They vary in
texture, size and architectural. They will however all have the same
trapezoid shape. Some only have one doorjamb and lintel, and some
have two. Some of the doors are simple and others have different security mechanisms such as stone rings, central trunks and other mechanisms, which served to tie together beams to make the doors more

secure. I think that the complex trapezoid shape of the doors might be a clue to at least one of them hiding something"

"Good advise Cordie." Bruce added and then turned with her to head toward the Temple of the Sun.

Bruce and Cordie followed the semi-circle shape of the temple. With the structure being an existing granite block shaped to blend with the natural curves it was unlikely that there would be any passage built into the solid rock. Still it was one of the most important building of Machu Picchu and they knew it had to be examined. There are two trapezoidal windows in the building. Both had protruding knobs at every corner, and on the north side there was one of Cordie's doors. It was a carefully sculpted door with bored holes in the doorjamb, very similar to the Qoricancha temple in Cusco. The slowly and deliberately ran their hands over every stone but found nothing.

Cordie finally gave up on the temple its self and led Bruce out toward the west. They stopped on a rectangular patio with nine ceremonial doorways alternating with prism-shaped studs.

"This is the Intiwatana it measured time (the solstice and the equinox) by using sunlight and shadow, and also served as an altar. In Quechua, "Inti" means "sun" and "Wata" means "year", thereby giving us the meaning of a solar year observatory." Codie explained.

Bruce looked around and saw that they were on a hill made up of several terraces. There were very well crafted steps leading to the Intiwatana. At the end of the staircase was the open patio where they stood. He could see an upper platform where a granite rock sculpted into three steps stood. He left Cordie examining the Intiwatana and climbed up to the platform. He stood in the central part looking directly at a rectangular prism about 35cm high. He was estimating at the height but what he was very sure of was that it was pointing from North-West to South-East. There had to be some significance to the fact that its four corners were directed to the four cardinal points.

Bruce was still contemplating the prism as he gazed across the ruins towards the dominant peak of Huana Picchu. The mists of the late morning cloud coverage were clearing and Bruce could clearly see the neatly terraced and sculpted terraces below its summit. Any people who could have accomplished such a graceful terracing on what were nearly vertical cliffs surely could have concealed an entrance to massive underground tunnels.

CHAPTER 25

Meanwhile Heath had led Denise and Amehd directly to the enormous leaning block of stone that holds up the Temple of the Sun. He pointed out to them the large crack in its bottom. Although it looked and had always been considered a natural crack in the stone it had been exceptionally decorated and furnished to be used as a tomb. In the doorway it shows a carving portraying the symbol of the goddess Mother Earth.

Heath had left Denise and Amehd examining the door and moved alone into the interior. Although he had been inside the tomb many times, this time he was looking at everything in a different way. He moved cautiously form niche-to-niche and monolithic pillar to monolithic pillar running his roughed hands over all of the stone. Then his hand finally felt it. He paused and retraced the path of his hand. Yes there was definitely something odd.

Denise had come up behind him. He took a hold of her hand saying, "here, run your hand along this wall. What do you feel?"

Denise did as Heath had instructed her and there definitely was a difference in what she felt. First she had felt the surface of the natural, uncut stone that the tomb was hued out of. Then almost without notice her hand had begun wiping along what had to be a series of perfectly fitted and polished interlocking cut stones. Then she was over their entirety and felt only the natural rock surface beneath her fingers again.

It was too dark to see the difference but she was fairly sure that she had felt the difference. A little concerned that if she said the wrong thing Heath would be unhappy with her, she took a deep breath and began cautiously. "I think there is a small section here in the wall that is made up of cut stones rather than the natural rock of the rest of the wall."

"Yes, that is what I thought too." Heath said thoughtfully. He took out a small light and began shining it directly where they had felt the difference in the stone. Even with the light it was almost impossible to see the lines that separated the natural wall with the carved stones. Still it was there, three perfectly fitted cut stones with nearly thirty angles each and interlocking faultlessly with the matching angle on the adjoining block.

"Watch the door Denise and send Amehd over here to help block the view incase anyone else comes in." Heath quickly ordered.

He continued to move his small pin light around the edges of the cut stones. There had to be some significant to this anomaly and he knew he could figure it out. Why would these stone be placed here in such an obscure manner? His mind was racing with questions as he stooped down and looked up the rock wall to get yet another view of the anomaly. Because of the multiple angles cut into each stone even the slightest variation in the angle of view gave a varied appearance to the person examining the cut stones.

Heath had been feeling around the stones and looking from every angle he could possibly position his line of vision for nearly two hours without saying a word. Amehd had finally had enough of his instructed role as sentry. Not another single tourist had even attempted to enter the tomb.

"Let me assist in examining the wall." Amehd finally spoke up to say.

Heath looked away from the wall for the first time since he had begun his examination. He didn't care very much for Amehd but he didn't seem to be finding any answers on his own. "Very well, here take my light."

Amehd took the small pin light from Heath's hand and began his own examination. To the complete frustration of Heath, it didn't take Amehd more than a few minutes to move his thin long brown fingers away from the cut rocks and trace an imaginary line from the most pre-dominate angle of the center block across the natural rock surface of the wall to the corner where the wall met the natural floor of the tomb. He knelt down in the dark corner and shined the pin light directly on a small opening in the rock.

Heath was infuriated that Amehd had done so effortlessly what he had not been able to do at all. He pushed the Egyptian out of the way and began to put his own fingers into the small opening.

Amehd shook his head at the barbarian behavior of this man he already detested. In his own very controlled manner Amehd picked himself up and shined the pin light down to assist Heath.

Heath felt inside the small opening with the index finger of his right hand. Just a few centimeters inside the opening he felt the distinctive feel of a solid stone lever. The smile of satisfaction on his face told Amehd that he had indeed found something inside the opening.

Without hesitation Heath pushed the lever down with his finger. It moved down effortlessly and Heath held it in the flattened position as the wall on the opposite corner of the tomb began to vibrate. Denise grabbed a hold of one of the pillars near where she was standing, as the floor seemed to begin trembling. Dust soon filled the tomb and it was quite impossible to see anything more than an inch or two in front of their own faces.

"Don't anyone move." Heath instructed as he removed his finger from the opening and pushed himself up to a standing position.

Denise was closest to the tomb opening so it was her vision that began to clear first. She couldn't believe her eyes. There where the corner of the natural rock wall had stood was an opening. The next thing she saw was Heath pushing his way past Amehd and through the dust still heavy at that end of the tomb as he moved directly toward the opening.

"Wait, Heath, we don't have any idea what is beyond there. Shouldn't we wait for the others?" Denise cried out before she had a chance to think better of it.

Heath completely ignored her and nearly ran the last few steps to the large opening now visible through the dust. There was a series of three very worn stone stares and then one of Cordie's doors. Heath wasn't waiting for anyone. He moved without hesitation down the steps and toward the hidden door.

Amehd moved cautiously up to the pillar where Denise stood. "Do you want to follow him or go after the others?" he asked calmly.

There was a quiver in Denise's voice as she replied. "I don't know. What do you think we should do Amehd?"

"I believe that at least one of us should follow him, just to make sure of what he discovers. However, if you prefer not to, I will go alone and you can go find Cordie and Bruce." Amehd replied sensibly.

"No, no that's alright. I think we should probably stay together and after all I should be getting pictures of what ever he finds. Surely it will be safe enough. I'm fine, lets go."

Just as Denise had stepped off the third and final stone step the opening behind the three disappeared. None of them had seen the natural stonewall move back in place, but it must have, there was no light now in the very small chamber they stood in facing the door. Heath pulled out his larger flashlight and immediately turned it on then instructed the other two to do the same thing.

Sparkles of emerald green and brilliant blue danced from where their lights fell on the door. It was a large complex trapezoid shaped door completely inlaid with the largest most luminous precious gemstones any of them had ever seen. There had to be at least a dozen each of the deep green emeralds, midnight blue sapphires and pure white diamonds all at least 40 carrots in size.

"My God would you look at these stones!" Heath said out loud.

There was a strange echo to his voice from the closeness of the walls of the small chamber they stood in. Still no one could move. The sight of such incredible beauty nearly had them all three mesmerized. It was Heath who soon realized though that the air was becoming stale. There wasn't any circulation or fresh air in the chamber. They were going to have to find a way to open the door or reopen the opening they had come through in the tomb.

From what they could tell the door seemed to have two doorjambs and lintels. He wasn't sure what the security mechanisms on the door were going to be, but he was fairly sure that a door hidden away in this manner would indeed have some kind of lock and protection from entering. Having Amehd and Denise shine their lights on the door Heath quickly began running his hands around it.

Denise was beginning to feel a little lightheaded and wondered why her breathing was becoming more difficult. Amehd and Heath both knew that they needed to get the door open very soon or they would all three run out of air to breath. Amehd joined in with Heath feeling every centimeter of the door.

Denise slowly dropped down to a sitting position. Her vision was even beginning to become a bit blurred and she didn't feel as if she could stand much longer. Amehd turned to make sure she was all right as Heath followed the direction of the beam of light from her flashlight that she had also lowered.

"Here look!" Heath called out as he stooped down and rubbed his fingers across what looked like a solid gold triangle set into the lower right hand corner of the door. As he pushed the golden triangle the door simply opened letting in an ample supply of fresh air.

On the other side of the door the air was curiously fresh and obviously circulating throughout the caverns that now lay out in front of them. It didn't take long for the fresh air to revive Denise and it finally occurred to her what had been happening. Amehd tried to comfort her and helped her back up to a standing position.

There were ancient writings and pictures along the cavern walls inside the door. Amehd couldn't read them clearly but it was pretty apparent to him that they were meant to warn off anyone who had made it this far. More specifically they seemed to warn off the uninitiated or unacquainted who might have made it this far. He knew that they should not be going in any further with out the whole group, but by this point he didn't have a whole lot of choice. Heath was already near the back of the cavern shining his flashlight around the walls.

"Look back here you two." Heath soon called out.

Amehd and Denise moved cautiously back toward the sound of his voice. There eyes were finally adjusting to the low light of the cavern and they couldn't believe what they saw laying out in front of them. Heath had found it and there was absolutely no way of denying it. There were a series of tunnels interconnected by sunken stairways beginning just a few steps ahead of where Heath stood. Even more astonishing the tunnels looked eerily familiar. They looked very similar to the massive underground labyrinth that they had followed Heath through back in Giza to find the crystal chamber.

There were but a couple of very significant differences between these Machu Picchu tunnels and those of Giza. The first and most easily apparent was the size. It looked as if this massive labyrinth, although on the same basic floor plan was at least double in size as what they had found in Giza. It had taken them nearly two hours to make their way to the crystal chamber in the Giza labyrinth so Amehd was already calculating that it might take them as much as four hours to find the center chamber here.

"We should not try to go on without Cordie and Bruce. We would not have ample time to find the chamber before we were scheduled to meet back up with them. Besides, they should be with us when we do find the chamber." Amehd said cautiously.

Heath simply ignored him as if he had not spoken at all. "Denise get me the ropes from your backpack. We are going ahead." Heath announced.

Denise and Amehd stood looking at each other in silence. They both knew that this was the wrong course of action but were powerless to stop Heath. As always, he was going to do things his way and caution of any kind was certainly not his way.

"Denise, I told you to get the ropes out. Now move, I want to get started." Heath yelled harshly back over his shoulder, still not taking his eyes off the sight of the massive labyrinth before him.

CHAPTER 26

Cordie set gazing across the ruins at the heavier cloud cover of white mist that had moved in over the peak of Huana Picchu. She realized that Machu Picchu really was a lost city in the clouds and that the clouds were like a mystical veil sometimes covering and sometimes revealing the whole of the area. It was disappointing that she and Bruce had found no evidence of any secret entrance in the temple or around any of the area they had explored. Still she could not help but enjoy soaking in the fantastic beauty of her surroundings.

"I hate to interrupt your thoughts Cordie," Bruce said with concern. "You look as if they are pleasant thoughts. Have you realized though that it is long past the time designated to regroup and we still haven't seen any sign of the others?'

Cordie looked down at her watch. Where had the time gone? Bruce was right it was several hours past time for the group to have gotten back together. The sun would be setting before long. What could have kept Heath and the others?

"I see, you are right Bruce. As much as I hate the idea of actually looking for Heath, I guess we should make our way down to the tomb area and see if we can find them." Cordie replied.

It didn't take long for Bruce and Cordie to find themselves inside the decorated crack in the foundation stone used as a tomb. It was unusually dusty inside and it looked like fresh dust with no fingerprints or evidence of anyone else having been in the tomb since it had settled. That was the first thing Cordie found unusual about the tomb. The second was that she found a small pin light lying very near the natural rock surface of one side of the tomb. She was sure it had belonged to Heath or one of their group. But how could any of them have been so careless to have lost it. If this were not a tourist site but a new dig that would result in contamination. Surely Heath and Amehd would have known better. Cordie assumed that it must have been Denise who would have committed such a serious violation in archaeological protocol as she picked up the penlight and dusted it off.

"Well they certainly are not still here in the tomb," Bruce observed. "What do you think we should do now?"

"Well, we have already missed the tourist train back to Cuzco. I suppose we should wait a bit longer to see if they show up and then if not." She paused as if she was thinking about what her next words should be. "I guess if they don't show up we should use your radio and call for a helicopter to fly in and pick us up. Hopefully they will show back up at the hotel in Cuzco."

Bruce considered her suggestion and although he didn't feel any more confident in it than she had sounded, he simply couldn't come up with any better plan of action. They both moved outside the tomb and found a comfortable place to set and watch the sun as it slowly began to set.

It was not long, not long at all before Heath became painfully aware of the second variation within the Machu Picchu labyrinth and those of Roslyn and Giza. He knew the horrifying instant that his foot had stepped on a stone in the walkway of the first tunnel that they had entered that he had triggered something. There had been a slight giving and an almost inaudible click as his left foot fell firmly on the trapezoidal stone beneath him.

"Drop to the ground and roll!" he shouted frantically as he was doing so himself.

Amehd saw that Denise was hesitating and immediately he understood that she did not know how to respond on instinct to Heath's
warning. He lunged forward pushing her out of the way just as a large
bundle of sharply pointed spears flung down and across the path
exactly where they stood.

Denise fell hard and had the wind temporarily knocked out of her.
The next thing she realized, Heath was pulling her further towards him.
He was holding her down next to the ground but pulling her at the
same time.

Denise didn't understand what had just happened. She was sore and
disorientated as Heath continued to drag her in a crawling fashion away
from where the spears had plunged deeply into the sidewall of the stone
tunnel. Then they stopped. Heath began to carefully and with very
deliberate movement rise slowly back to a standing position.

Denise saw the look of terror on his face as he looked back in the
direction they had come. She couldn't help herself and allowed her own
vision to follow his line of site.

"Oh my God!" she whaled out in horror as she saw the lifeless body
of Amehd hanging pined to the cold stonewall. He had been completely
impaled by at least two of the spears. One pieced through his chest near
his heart, which probably resulted in his very quick death, while the second rested in the upper portion of his right thigh.

There was blood dripping from both his wounds and his mouth.
Insects had already begun to appear and climb on the body and in the
pools of blood. Denise went into an immediate state of shock. She
couldn't move or take her eye off the horror before her.

Heath grabbed her wrist and pulled her up to a standing position. He
forcibly turned her body to face him and put her back toward Amehd's
body. She was beginning to tremble and tears were falling freely from
her eyes.

"Straighten up, you hear me Denise. You have to get a hold of yourself."
Heath demanded as he shook her in an effort to refocus her attention. He

knew that she was going in to shock. He didn't have time to deal with her falling apart on him. There were sure to be more traps between him and the treasure and he had to keep his mind focused.

"He pushed me out of the way. He knew it was coming and saved me instead of himself." She mumbled now more fully in a state shock and horror.

"Don't think about that right now. Denise can you hear me? Do you understand what I am saying to you? We have to be very careful now. This place is booby trapped and if we don't both want to end up like Amehd then you have to do exactly as I tell you." Heath said very sternly.

Once he believed that he actually had Denise's attention Heath told her he was going to let go of her shoulders. "I need to get Amehd's back pack, there are things in there that we will need. Now you must stand perfectly still. Do you understand me Denise. Don't move a single step."

"You can't just leave him there like that." Denise shouted in a revived tone of urgency. "You can't leave Amehd hanging there from those stakes!"

Heath turned to look back over his shoulder at Denise. He stared with a calm fascination that seemed to scare Denise even more than she already was. "We can't try to move him. We don't have any idea what other traps moving him might trigger. Besides, the man is dead and we can't do anything for him. We have to think about ourselves right now."

Heath eased his way gingerly up as close to Amehd's body as he could without touching any of the sharply carved stakes. Already there was the constant buzzing hum of flies being attracted to the still body by the blood. Amehd's mouth and eyes were open. His white teeth were now covered with a dark sticky red coating of drying blood and his eyes glared hollow and empty as Heath moved in to unbuckle the straps of his backpack.

The low vibration of the constant buzzing noise from the large black flies was almost hypnotic. Heath tried to push the torment of both the sounds and the sights attacking him out of his mind and concentrate solely on removing the backpack trapped between Amehd's lifeless body and the dirt and stone of the labyrinth wall.

It was nearly 11:30 pm by the time that Cordie and Bruce gave up on any of Heath's group showing back up. They had called for a helicopter that flew right in and picked them up. They weren't nearly as worried at this point about keeping a low profile. Right now all they could think about was what might have happened to the others.

It surprised Cordie that as she tried to fall asleep she worried not only about Heath, but the empty bed that Denise should be sleeping in. Surely Heath would not have allowed anything to happen to them.

CHAPTER 27

Heath had kept Denise moving all night long. She was still numb from both the physical pain of the fall she had taken and the emotional turmoil she felt over Amehd's death. All she could feel was the dryness in her mouth and how tired her legs were. Because of the caution Heath took in leading them through the labyrinth while not setting off any more deadly traps, it had taken them nearly nine hours to reach the inner chamber. Heath could see his watch only when he pushed the small button on one side to light up the face. He knew that Bruce and Cordie must be missing them by now.

"Look Denise, we are finally here," he announced as they reached a familiar stone door. This inner door was nothing like the more elaborate doors of Machu Picchu. Instead it was a completely unassuming solid stone door very much like the ones at Roslyn and Giza.

Heath was as exhausted as Denise was and wasn't at all sure that he would be able to open the door on his own. He remembered how it had taken the assistance of both Bruce and Adam to open the Giza door. He paused and took a bottle of water from Amehd's backpack.

"Here take a drink and catch your breath. I may need your help in opening this door." Heath said to Denise showing little emotion.

The water was not cold but it still felt good to Denise. She drank as much as Heath would allow and then replaced the screw on top. She took her own backpack off and set it down along the wall by the door.

She didn't know how much help she was going to be able to be, but she just wanted to get this all over with and get out of these tunnels.

To Heath's amazement and relief the door pushed open almost effortlessly. Just as in Giza as soon as there was a crack in the door a bright light shown through. He looked at Denise and smiled.

Heath entered the inner chamber and in the center of the perfectly hued rock chamber rested a gold wedge shaped type of rod. It seemed to rest in a covering of brilliant bright white light similar to what the crystals had originally given off. It looked as if the wedge was a part of a sundial type devise resting directly in the center of the solid stone chamber.

Heath slowly moved toward the devise and ran his hand through the bright light and close enough to the rod to make sure it wasn't putting off any great degree of heat. As his hand neared the light faded and there was no heat coming from the golden rod. He effortlessly grabbed it and pulled it up away from the rest of the devise. As soon as the rod was no longer touching any other part of the golden sundial like devise embedded in the stone floor, the light disappeared completely.

Heath Conrad stood holding what he believed was probably the single most valuable thing he had ever held in his hands. He knew by the feel that this rod was most likely just as pure gold as the stands the crystals had rested on had been. He had it, the final piece to the puzzle. He had the Golden Wedge.

Morning dawned back in Cuzco still with no word or sign of Heath and his group. Cordie was drinking her second cup of coca tea in the lobby near the fireplace when Bruce appeared in the hotel entrance. He had already been out making inquiries about renting the services of a helicopter for the day to search along the Inca trail and the whole complex of Machu Picchu for the rest of his group.

"It has occurred to me Cordie," Bruce began quietly as he set down beside her, "if by some means Heath did find his way into the tunnels yesterday, it would not be out of character for him to proceed on his own. If that is the case, then perhaps just as we did in Giza they may exit at a different location than the exact spot they entered. I think our best course of action today will be to search from the air and see if we can locate them coming out."

Cordie was extremely impressed with how well Bruce was handling things. She whole-heartedly agreed with him and added, "Yes, we entered through the Great Pyramid tunnel but came back out near the Sphinx. That is a very sound hypothesis Bruce. If we correlate the tomb to the Great Pyramid then where would the Sphinx be located?

"I have already worked that out. Amehd would probably be more accurate with this than I am but I believe it will be somewhere in this vicinity of the Incan Trail." Bruce pointed to the spot on a small map he had with him.

Denise had not gone into the chamber with Heath. She stood in place outside the door rubbing her tired legs trying desperately not to allow the image of poor Amehd to sneak back into her mind. She had never seen anything so horrible in her life, and hoped she never would again.

"Denise, come on we have it." Heath said triumphantly as he emerged from the chamber. He picked up her backpack took out some soft cloth and wrapped the golden rod. "Here put this as deep down into my pact as you can," he instructed her.

"It shouldn't take us nearly as long to get back out as it did to come in. I doubt that they would have booby trapped the return route, but we'll want to be careful just the same." Heath said as he stood allowing Denise to put the golden rod down into his backpack.

The helicopter pilot had been circling the radius that Bruce had marked out for him on the map. It was now late morning and if they didn't find what they were looking for soon he had informed Bruce that they would have to return to Cuzco to refuel.

Cordie searched from one side of the helicopter while Bruce did the same from the other. They had been at it for hours and there was still no sign what so ever of Heath, Amehd and Denise. Then suddenly Bruce called out over the noise of the helicopter.

He was pointing for Cordie to look down at a clearing in the lower part of the Inca Trail as it left Machu Picchu.

It took her a few minutes to adjust her eyes to what Bruce had thought he saw. Then she saw it too. It looked like Heath and Denise resting along the side of the trail. They didn't see Amehd but they could clearly see the Legacy House makers on the three backpacks setting beside the two.

Bruce worked out a landing strategy with the pilot and within a few minutes they were on the ground just a few feet from Heath and Denise.

They had not gone far along the trail after emerging from a rocky crevice along the Inca Trail. Denise was having trouble with her eyes adjusting to the bright light of day above ground. Heath had agreed to rest and give her a chance to wash out her eyes with a cloth and some fresh water. As soon as they heard the helicopter and saw that it was coming in for a landing, Heath and Denise both knew that Cordie and Bruce must have found them.

Heath told Bruce what had happened and how Amehd had died as Cordie tried to assist Denise who was still not in very good condition. She seemed to be suffering from shock and exhaustion and surprisingly Cordie felt a great deal of compassion for the young woman.

CHAPTER 28

By the afternoon of the second day Felix knew that he would not have a lot of time and he must begin preparing Adam. He finished examining and he thought deciphering another group of petrogtyphs from along the strange corridor. He was fairly sure by this point that the corridor was not going to be a part of their experience in the cave. He believed that they had indeed found the fabled Seven Caves and that the corridor was a path used when a select few of the population of the earth needed to be saved from an impending catastrophe, such as a meteorite strike or the great flood.

Putting everything he knew together Felix now understood that the most ancient civilization of the world had been made up of both humans and angels that worked together to use the knowledge God gave them to survey and map the earth and stars of the material universe. They had devised a way to predict the displacement in the earth's crust and the coming of such catastrophic events that would wipe out life on the earth. It was through the corridor that only a chosen few of each great time were saved and sheltered until it was time to teach the natives of the repopulated earth the ways of civilization and knowledge of the sciences all over again. Those few saved each time were the shinning ones.

It was not yet time for an end to come. They had not been brought here to travel through the corridor. Felix knew that for sure. Their adventure would take place among the center chamber of the cave and within each of the seven lobes of that chamber. It was time now though that Felix start trying to explain the Gnostic heritage to Adam so when it did begin, he would understand what was happening. It was easy to see that Adam and Gabriella were growing closer and closer. It may also be needed that Felix begin preparing Adam to become his son-in-law and a watcher in the Legacy House. Felix smiled at the thought.

"Grandfather you look like you are thinking of something very pleasant." Gabriella said shaking him free from his solitary thoughts.

"Yes, very pleasant indeed young one," Felix replied warmly. "Where has Adam gone?"

Gabriella set down on a pallet beside her grandfather and put her hand in his. She smiled that intoxicating smile of hers and finally answered his question. "He went out to scout around the cave. I actually asked him to give you and I a little time alone together this afternoon."

"What has caused me to deserve such attention from my beautiful young granddaughter?" Felix asked as he patted her hand.

"I had hoped we could talk about Adam. Oh grandfather, I think that I am in love with him. Please tell me that you approve and think he could fit into the Legacy House." Her voice echoed with a mixture of joy and fear.

"I do approve of Adam, Gabriella dear." Felix saw the immediate relief in her face as he continued speaking. "You know that he will have to be told of the obligations of your heritage and the role he and your children would be required to fill as watchers."

Gabriella joyfully kissed her grandfather's cheek then responded. "I know he will understand and accept it. I just know that he will. I can't explain it grandfather, but it is as if I have know Adam my entire life."

"I feel pretty sure that he will as well dear, but you know I will have to talk with him." Felix hesitated and then in a melancholy tone added, "It should be your father having this talk with Adam you know. I did my duty in initiating your mother to our heritage. We are each only supposed to have to do that once in our lifetimes. I still do not understand why your parents were taken from us so early in their lives."

"Nor do I grandfather, but you know that God had his reasons and it is not for us to always understand." Gabriella replied wisely.

Felix wiped a small tear from his granddaughters face. He smiled warmly and reassured her that he would talk to Adam yet today.

By the time Adam returned to the cave it was nearly dusk. He had gathered a fine collection of wild berries to add to the evening meal.

"I can't believe how thick the mosquitoes and other insects get as the afternoon cools off out side this cave," Adam said as he entered the cave.

"Well, then aren't we lucky to have this cave as shelter." Gabriella said cheerfully as she took the berries from him.

"That may very well be true for reasons far more significant than you yet realize." Felix added.

"It sounds as if you have figured out something worth sharing," Adam replied as he rubbed more of the insect repellant over his exposed skin.

Gabriella turned to look in the direction of her grandfather. She wondered how much he would tell Adam or if that was even what he was about to do. Felix only looked up and gave her a reassuring wink.

CHAPTER 29

Gabriella and Adam were becoming accustomed to waking naturally to the soft warm rays of the sun lighting up the cave from the front skylight each morning. They had spent nearly all of the last full day and a half setting at Felix's feet listening to him recount the knowledge of the Gnostic ways and the responsibility of the Watchers of the Legacy House. Adam seemed to absorb the wonders and mysterious intrigue that surrounded Gabriella with little effort. Felix was becoming even surer that Adam had some ancient connection or ancestral gift that connected him to the voice of the ancient conscience.

It was the fourth day since the others had left, but Adam felt as if a lifetime had passed. He was viewing nearly everything from a slightly different perspective and he liked how it felt. He knew that he was truly falling in love with Gabriella and her whole family and way of life. He couldn't wait to wake up in the morning and begin each day with Gabriella and Felix.

Neither Bruce nor Cordie had said a word to Heath since they had boarded the Legacy House jet. They were both still appalled that he had led Amehd to his death and made no attempt to retrieve his body. Denise still wasn't dealing with what she had seen very well. She almost set motionless in either a dazed state or with silent tears rolling down her face. Cordie wished there was something more that she could do for her.

Heath looked out the side window of the jet as the sun rose over the eastern horizon and they sped closer and closer back toward the Seven Caves. Finally the small island was coming into view below them.

"We'll be landing soon. Do you have our papers in order?" Heath said coldly to Bruce.

Bruce looked at Cordie and their mutual detest for the man showed clearly on their faces. He may have retrieved the Golden Wedge, but it had been at the cost of a man's life and neither of them were ready to let that fact go unrecognized or forgotten.

It had taken something so tragic as the loss of Amehd's life and seeing the emotional scares inflicted on Denise to wake Cordie up. Finally, after so many years of first hiding from her feelings then bouncing back an fourth from lustful desire to an honest loathing could see Heath Conrad for the reckless man she should have always known he was. For the first time in her life, Cordie could look at him and know that he had no power what so ever over her feelings.

He did unfortunately still have some influence on the next day or so of her immediate life in that he was the one in possession of the Golden Wedge. Because of that fact and that fact alone it was Cordie who finally gave Heath a verbal response.

"Bruce has handled everything. We will go directly through customs and be on the road back toward the cave as soon as we land." There was neither warmth nor anger in her voice. She had simply stated the facts.

It was late morning when Adam heard the sounds of someone approaching the cave entrance. He knew that it would either be some of the military patrol of the area, or the rest of their group returning. For just a moment Adam almost wished it to be a military officer checking in on their expedition. They had the proper permits and after all if it were a military officer, he probably wouldn't stick around long. Adam was so enjoying the private time he and Gabriella were having with Felix.

There was a definite mixed feeling when Adam finally saw Codie entering the main cavern of the cave. Felix on the other hand seemed immediately alarmed. Somehow he knew that something had gone terribly wrong.

The old man began to shake and tremble. He set down to hide the severity of his condition. By the time Bruce came in with Denise on his arm Cordie had already gone to kneel down in front of Felix.

Heath stood silently holding his pack with the Golden Wedge inside as Cordie told Felix of Amehd's fate. Gabriella turned and buried her face in Adam's chest at the news. Bruce saw the tears welling up in Felix's old and tired eyes and wished desperately that he could have done something to protect his grandfather from such pain.

It was several minutes later before Felix spoke. He knew that he did not have the strength left to stand without showing how his hands were still trembling. He remained seated with both hands cupped in his lap. "So we are seven now. You did retrieve the Golden Wedge then?" he said in the weakest voice Bruce had ever heard come from the old man.

Heath stepped forward and carefully took the Golden Wedge from his pack. He stooped down and handed the relic to Felix, still not saying a word.

CHAPTER 30

Gabriella laid awake most of the night. She didn't like being so far removed from Adam or her grandfather. No one in the group had questioned Felix when he positioned the Golden Wedge precisely in the spot where a dais would have set in ancient times under the front skylight. He then followed the angular line from the three corners of the wedge and without effort found exactly where each of the three crystal keys was to set. It had not been until he had explained that each of the seven of the group would have to sleep in one of the separate seven lobes off the main cave cavern that anyone had questioned him.

Cordie was not concerned for herself, but she wasn't sure that Denise was in any shape yet to be expected to sleep alone in one of the isolated lobes of the cave. Felix explained very patiently that it had to be so. The first morning rays of the sun would filter in and activate the Golden Wedge. The Golden Wedge would then reflect the power of the sun to activate the crystal keys. They each had to be in their own isolated portion of the cave to await the lifting of the veil between the two universes.

Gabriella knew that she probably had a better understanding of what to expect than anyone else in the group, with the obvious exception of Felix. Still she simply could not sleep waiting for the darkness of the night to pass. She wondered if it was that she just missed knowing that Adam was sleeping only a few feet away from her as he had been every since they had arrived in the cave. No, she did miss Adam's closeness, but she knew that the next few hours were going to bring such revelations and she only hoped she would be able to understand them.

The soft pink and lavender rays of the breaking sun finally began to dance their magic as the sun rose over the Isle of Youth just off the coast of Cuba. No one said a word as they each waited breathlessly and silent within their own assigned lobe of the Seven Caves. Just as Felix had somehow understood the rays of the sun gave power to the Golden Wedge. Bright lightning like streaks of energy flew from each of the three corners of the wedge hitting precisely each of the marvelous crystal keys. An ever-increasing ring of energy began to explode like the many ripples of water after a droplet had fallen. Each series of rings of pure white energy continued to expand in an ever widening range until finally each of the seven lobes of the cave were bathed within the brilliance of the rings of light.

Felix immediately felt the glorious freedom of his soul being lifted from the weight of his old and failing body. He floated up still bathed in the security of the rings of energy that lifted him. He could look back down and clearly see the other six lobes and his six companions. He didn't have to look up or out to feel the presents of all those greeting him from the other side of the veil. He wasn't seeing them with his eyes or any real kind of sight at all. It was just a presents that he felt and knew without a doubt that he was surrounded with love.

"Father, we have waited so long for you to arrive." Again it wasn't exactly that he was hearing in the same way that a human would actually hear someone speak. Yet he felt the words coming from within the sparkles of pure spiritual beings that now surrounded him completely.

There were no words in any of the languages that Felix had ever learned that could adequately explain the feeling of connection and belonging that he now felt. The joy and peace seemed to be infused within all of the beings around him and Felix knew that he was not only in the presents of his son and daughter-in-law once again, but that all who had ever come before him during all the ages of the earth were apart of his being. So much was finally made crystal clear to his soul. He understood so much and felt a powerful sense of peace that seemed to penetrate every vibration surrounding him.

It was Bruce whose soul next joined the collective. He had been lifted up leaving his own body to rest on the cave floor. It was not a feeling of being forcibly sucked from the shell of his human body as much as it was an escape. He felt as if the door had been opened and he was allowed to fly free from his cage.

He knew that his grandfather was present, but he also understood that both his mother and father's souls were wrapping their presents around him. Almost at the same time Gabriella's fresh loving soul was also present. There was even more of a bond between Bruce and Gabriella than they had felt in flesh. Their souls seemed to almost be rejoined as one. It was not a brotherly sisterly kind of joining that twins might normally feel, nor was it a kind of joining that lovers might feel. It was simply as if their souls were closer to one soul that had been split apart for some unexplained reason and now had the opportunity to feel whole again.

"God has protected and guarded humankind since the time of Seth. He has nurtured the Gnostic, knowledge and special acquaintance with him directly that only the children and descendants of Seth hold deep within the make up of their souls." Again the explanation wasn't actually being given to them in the form of speech, it was more just feeling the words rather than hearing them. Somehow they realized that the senses they had depended on, as humans were so limited and weak. It was as if they had been blind and could now see, but seeing wasn't just a site it was a presents.

"There are other very special souls on earth in the material universe that the descendants of Japheth and Sham that can be led into finding and accepting that same very special acquaintance and knowledge of

God. You have two such souls with you. Are you ready for them to be lifted through the veil?"

Within moments Adam and Cordie simultaneously felt the same freedom of their souls being lifted from the stifling prison of their earthly bodies. Soon they were also a part of the spiritual consciousness existing on the other side of the thin veil separating the spiritual and material universes. Suddenly all five could clearly understand what was not conceivable by the limitations of their human minds. Things they in human form had never endeavored to contemplate became crystallized from within the depths of their souls.

For Cordie it was the immediate understanding that God had forgiven her for turning her back on her vows to become a nun. God didn't care about such things as holy orders or dogmatic church structures. God had never felt that she had in any way turned her back on him, only on the creations of man that used His being to keep other humans in line. The relief she felt was like being reborn and if that in itself were not enough Cordie then felt the presents of the soul of her own earthly mother. She had never felt that she belonged and now she overwhelmingly felt that she had never not belonged. Cordie courageously reached out from deep within the most broken places in her soul to embrace the soul of her earthly mother. It was an experience of the most significant magnitude that some how seemed to heal all her past pains.

The preparations that Felix had given Adam were very helpful. Still nothing could have prepared him for the complete peace and security of being, that he suddenly felt. It was as if he and Gabriella were somehow experiencing the true joining of their souls emits the protection and comfort of all the shining souls of heaven. It was as if time stood still or as if there was no such thing as time all at once.

Gabriella and Adam were immediately confronted with a whirlwind of past sensations and they both realized that this was not the first lifetime that their souls had shared. So much became clear as they were reminded of their lives together as Amir and Adar concealing the great pillar of knowledge beneath the ground of the lush green jungle that once stood where the sands of Egypt are now found. Glimpses of their lives together as Gitta and Dermot, Anelique and Anton and even Maria and Johann became a part of their conscious memories.

"You have all done well my children" again all five of them understood and felt more than actually heard what was being told them. "You have pieced together some of the most ancient clues left throughout the crevasse of your material universe in a large degree because you were willing to listen to the holy spirit within each of you and believe in what you felt in your hearts. The last time that angles or watchers directly from our spiritual universe surveyed the material creations of your planet was in fact when they took Enoch on his journey.

Although Enoch was not of the sons of Seth his soul was acquainted and he found enlightenment during a time leading up to the last great flood. He understood that purity of mind and therefore true acquaintance with God was always present and he only had to clear the ways of the material universe from his mind to be awakened. Like the five of you, he was shown in clarity what lied in great mystery for the rest of humankind.

The material universe and the human bodies that Ialdabaoth, the false God of so many humans, created to imprison your real being, your souls, lasts for only a short period. His further curse of imprisonment upon you while in the material universe is what you have come to call your Destiny. Great heavenly saviors of the human soul have we sent to teach. They walked among you in the same stifling prisons and were known as Jesus, Buddha and a great many other names. Each was a reincarnation of a preexistent Christ, a preexistent Word, a preexistent Seth, or Barbelo. Each did their small part to teach human kind how to escape the influence of the malevolent rulers, but the hold of Ialdabaoth over his domain of the material universe as he created it is very strong.

Nothing of the material universe is purely good nor is it purely evil. Ialdabaoth is merely what he is, morally ambivalent. He and his rulers of the material side enslave through the use of a malevolent spirit of deception. You, the offspring of light of Seth or the awakened soul have the opportunity to respond to a good spirit that has been bestowed through your heritage or your desire for acquaintance. According to how each soul responds and gains that acquaintance, you either escape and return here to God and this spiritual universe, or you become reincarnated in another body.

Spirituality and the personal acquaintance of each soul is not to be dictated by any denomination or religion created by humankind. Whether it go by the name of Gnostic, Essecs of Qumran, Buddhaism, Hinduism, The Baha'I Faith, Christianity, Islam, Judaism, Taoism, Zoroastrianism or any one of the other many names it has been call, all of the religions of the material world have been in some way contaminated by the malevolent spirit of deception of humankind. It is the spirituality or connectedness and acquaintance of the soul that transcends the separation of those religious distinctions."

The longer their souls hovered in the shining presents of the spiritual world the more each of the group understood. It was as if what ever the most important question in their own existence had been, the spirit of heaven knew and answered. God allowed them a unique understanding.

"No the soul of Amehd is not with us now. He was here briefly after his noble behavior to save the life of the one you know as Denise. He was reincarnated back and although he has come much closer to an awaken understanding he was still held back by many of his traditional Egyptian beliefs. His bondage will not be many more lifetimes."

Adam though of his desire for Gabriella and instantly he felt the blessings of all of heaven on their union and knew that they were to be married and have a wonderfully large family during this lifetime.

"There is no such relationship as man and wife, brother and sister or even mother and father here in heaven. We all just are and exist in our most spiritual state. But we honor the needs of the material world you live in and send you back assured that your marriage will be a blessed one."

With the realization of those last thoughts, Cordie and Bruce felt themselves beginning to be pulled back down through the veil separating the worlds. It was not a fearful feeling; they continued to carry back to the material universe the completeness they had achieved from their transportation to heaven. Still it was a feeling of being forcibly stuffed back into their human bodies.

There was a delay before Gabriella and Bruce were released. They knew that Felix would not be returning to the material universe with them. It was as if they were given a special moment or so to adjust themselves to the realization.

"Do not be sad for me children. As you like no others can see, I am finally free of the prison of the material universe and you both know now that I am always here and in contact with the holy spirit within your own souls. Rejoice for my freedom and that I have achieved Ati, our great perfection."

It deeply saddened Bruce, but in some small, deeply buried part of her consciousness Gabriella knew that Felix would be with her again. She didn't know what it was but she knew he would not really be gone forever.

Suddenly the rings of energy disappeared from within the cave. Bruce, Gabriella, Adam and Cordie slowly felt the need of their human body to breath and take in air again. It was a painful and wretched feeling in comparison with the bliss their freed souls had felt. It was as if they each felt foreign or misplaced for the first few minutes as their souls reacquainted themselves with the burden of their physical bodies commanding the blood to begin to flow through there veins and their hearts to pump once again.

"Nothing, Not a God Damn Thing!" Heath was bellowing out in the main cavern of the cave. His face was red with furry and tormented disappointment.

Bruce and Adam both jumped to their feet and ran out to where Heath stood in the center cavern of the Seven Caves. The Golden Wedge was gone. Nothing stood on the floor where they had watched Felix place it. None of the three crystals remained in the holders. There was nothing but the emptiness of the center cavern.

"What has happened? Why didn't it work and where has everything gone?" Heath was nearly in a fit as he was running from where each of the crystals had been placed. He finally dropped down on the dirt flooring where the pure gold wedge shaped devise he had carried back from Peru had been placed.

By this time Cordie, Gabriella and Denise were also all standing back out in the center cavern of the cave. Cordie looked at Denise. She could now see the lost young woman who had been led astray by the overwhelming ways of the world and this wretched man they had both loved. She now felt a great need, almost an overwhelming sensation to reach out and help this woman she had so disliked only a few days ago. Cordie felt infused with the wisdom, power and truths that had been shown her and she wanted desperately to help Denise as she asked her very tenderly, "Did you experience anything Denise?"

"No, just a flash of light that didn't last more than a fraction of a second and then I heard Heath yelling about it not working." She replied honestly.

Cordie looked knowingly at the others and smiled with a new sense of peace and understanding in her heart. Her grin of satisfaction was not wasted on Adam or Bruce, but Gabriella seemed to be still reflecting on the revelations of their experience. It was Bruce then that stepped in and took charge. He explained that Felix had died and asked Adam to help carry his body back to the jet. They both knew it was only a shell of what Felix had been imprisoned in, but they had to keep up appearances.

Heath couldn't understand how Bruce had known that Felix was dead. He had not gone into the side lobe where Felix lay prior to making the announcement. He also couldn't understand how everyone else seemed to be able to just accept the failure of the morning. Not only had they not been led to any great treasure but he had even somehow lost the gold and crystal that he had already found. What had all of this been for? Where was his reward, his riches?

No one ever knew what had happened to the Golden Wedge, the crystals or the pure gold stand that had also mysteriously vanished from the Cairo Legacy House. Heath raved for years trying to get anyone to listen to his incredible story about tunnels under major sacred sites across the globe all holding precious treasures. Unfortunately for him, Denise refused to provide him with any photographic proof and he was never able to find the entrances to any of the three sites again.

Adam and Gabriella were married and took up residence in the Cairo Legacy House where Jamila was still living and able to hold their first-born son in her mothering arms. Bruce took up a leading role in the Scotland Legacy House and stayed in close touch with Cordie who after changing major aspects of her class material had been accepted back at the university in New York. Her new work on proving the level of sophisticated knowledge of ancient civilizations led her to a great deal of prestige and respect among a previously unyielding populous of academics.

All of their lives and what they would give to the world of the material universe while imprisoned here on earth had been changed forever.